William Henry Giles Kingston

A Tale of the Shore and Ocean

Or, the heir of Kilfinnan

William Henry Giles Kingston

A Tale of the Shore and Ocean
Or, the heir of Kilfinnan

ISBN/EAN: 9783337027186

Printed in Europe, USA, Canada, Australia, Japan

Cover: Foto ©Andreas Hilbeck / pixelio.de

More available books at **www.hansebooks.com**

DENHAM SAVED FROM THE SHARK.

A TALE OF THE

SHORE AND OCEAN;

OR,

THE HEIR OF KILFINNAN.

BY

WILLIAM H. G. KINGSTON,

AUTHOR OF "HENDRICKS THE HUNTER," "DICK CHEVELEY," "THE TWO SUPERCARGOES," ETC., ETC.

ILLUSTRATED.

NEW YORK:
A. C. ARMSTRONG & SON,
714 BROADWAY.
1881.

PREFACE.

THE following tale contains materials for a full-sized novel, but my readers probably will not object to have them condensed into a single modest volume.

The scene of a considerable portion of the story is laid on the coast of Ireland, where the peasantry mostly speak the native Irish, and I have therefore translated what my characters say into ordinary English rather than into the generally received brogue, which would be, coming from their lips, as inappropriate as Spanish or Dutch.

When English is spoken, it sounds somewhat highflown, but is certainly purer than the language of the same class in England. Thus, my hero talks more like a well-educated young gentleman than a humble fisher lad. If that is considered a defect, I hope that it may be redeemed by the stirring incidents with which the tale abounds, and that old and young may alike find as much amusement as they expect in its perusal.

W. H. G. K.

A TALE OF THE SHORE AND OCEAN.

CHAPTER I.

THE west coast of Ireland presents scenery of the most beautiful and romantic character. Here grey peaks rise up amidst verdure of emerald green; trees of varied hue come feathering down close to the water; yellow sands line the shores of many lonely bays; dark rocks of fantastic shape extend out into the ocean, while deep blue lochs mirror on their bosoms the varied forms of the surrounding heights.

On the south-west part of the coast a wide bay is to be found. At the extreme southern end, up a deep loch, a castle, the seat of an ancient family, reared its towers high above the waters. The bay came sweeping round at some places with a hard sandy beach; then, again, the ground rose, leaving but a narrow ledge between the foot of the cliffs and the waters. Thus the shore extended on for some distance, forming a lofty headland, when it again sank to its former level. A reef of rocks ran

out a considerable distance into the ocean, forming a natural breakwater to the bay. Here and
there to the north were several deep indenta-
tions, in which fishing-boats and several coasting
craft might find shelter. In some of these little
bays fishermen had formed their habitations, mostly
out of the wrecks of stout ships which had been
cast on their rocky shores. In some of the coves
or bays several huts had been congregated together, but a short distance north of the promontory which has been spoken of stood a single hut.
It was strongly built of ships' timbers and roofed
with stout planks, kept down by heavy stones, so
that, though the furious blasts which swept across
the Atlantic blew against it, it had hitherto with-
stood the rough shocks to which it had been
exposed.

The day was lovely; not a cloud dimmed the
blue heavens, while the sun setting over the distant
ocean shed a glow of light across the waters,
rippled by a gentle westerly breeze. Several boats
were approaching the shore. In one of them sat a
lad. No other person was to be seen on board.
The dark nets were piled up in the centre of the
boat, at the bottom of which a number of fish, still
giving signs of life, showed that he had been successful in his calling. Every now and then he

looked up at the tanned sail to see that it drew properly, and then would cast his eye towards the shore to watch the point to which he was steering. He could scarcely have numbered twelve summers, though his figure was tall and slight. His trousers were rolled up above the knees, showing his well-turned legs and feet. His shirt sleeves were treated in the same manner, while the collar thrown back, exhibited his broad and well-formed chest. His eyes were large and dark, and the hue of his skin gave indication that Spanish blood was flowing in his veins; while his dark locks escaping from beneath his fisherman's red cap, gave a still more southern look to his well-chiseled features. His practical knowledge and activity seemed to have made up for his want of strength, for few boys of his age would have ventured forth to sea in a fishing-boat of that size by themselves. Another and a larger boat had been for some time steering a course to approach him.

"Ah! Dermot, me darlin'; and all alone too?" said a man from the boat which now overtook him.

"Yes! my mother was ill and unable to go off, so I went by myself; an' see, Uncle Shane, I have had a good haul for my pains."

"I see, boy, an' sure I'm glad of it," said the first speaker; "but you are scarcely strong enough to go off alone, for should a gale spring up you would be unable to manage that boat by yourself."

"Och! an' haven't I managed her before now in heavy weather?" replied Dermot. "But suppose, Uncle Shane, I was lost, would you take care of my mother? She's not so strong as she used to be; toil has worn her down, working hard for me when I ought to have been toiling for her."

"I will," answered Shane.

"Will you swear it, uncle, by the Holy Virgin and the blessed saints?"

"I will, Dermot, as I hope for mercy in the day of trouble. But why do you ask that question?"

"Because, uncle, as I was pulling up my nets I slipped and almost fell overboard. I thought that had my feet been entangled, as they might have been, I should have gone down an' been unable to regain the boat. We none of us know what may happen; but could I feel that my mother would be protected from want, it would nerve my arm, and make me feel more ready for whatever lot may be in store for me."

"Boy," observed the elder fisherman, looking at his nephew, "you are thoughtful above your years; but the saints will protect you, and I will not forget to make an offering to St. Nicholas, that he may watch over you."

Thus conversing the old man and the lad steered their boats towards the shore side by side, the former hauling in his mainsail somewhat to lessen the speed of his boat. They parted to the northward of the promontory described, Dermot steering for the little cove in which stood the solitary hut already spoken of, while his uncle continued along the shore a little further to the north.

Dermot ran his boat between two rocks, at the end of which was a small sandy beach, where a capstan being placed he was enabled to haul her up out of the water. As he approached, a woman was seen descending from the hut. The same dark eyes and raven hair, though somewhat streaked with white in her case, which characterized the boy, was observable in the woman. Her figure was thin and wiry, giving indication of the severe toil to which she was exposed. She was dressed in a rough frieze petticoat, with a dark handkerchief drawn across her bosom, and the usual red cloak and hood worn at that time by most of the peasantry of the west of Ireland was thrown over her shoulders.

"Mother!" exclaimed the boy, "see, I have done well; I have had a better haul than we have got for many a day."

"And maybe, Dermot, we will have a better

market too," observed the woman. "It is said the Earl has come to the castle with many fine people, and they will be wanting fish to a certainty. It would be too late now to go, they would not see you; but to-morrow morning, as soon as the sun is up, you shall set forth, and to be sure they'll be glad to buy fish of my Dermot." The woman drew herself up as she spoke, and looked towards the boy with a glance of pride, as if she would not exchange him for any of the highest born in the land.

"How are you, mother?" asked Dermot; "have all those aches of which you were complaining gone away? Do you feel strong again?"

"Yes; the saints were merciful; I did not forget to pray to them, and they have heard me," answered the woman.

With her, as with most of her countrywomen, superstition, if it had not altogether taken the place of religion, had been strangely mixed up with it; yet she spoke in a tone of simple and touching faith, at which no one with any feeling would have ventured to sneer.

Next morning, Dermot, laden with the finest of his fish in a basket at his back, set off along the shores of the bay towards Kilfinnan Castle. The approach to it was wild and picturesque. A narrow estuary, having to be crossed by a bridge, almost isolated the castle from the mainland, for the ground on which the old fortress stood was merely joined to it by a rugged and nearly impassable ledge of rocks. The castle itself was of considerable size and strongly built, so that it could well withstand the gales which, from time to time, circled round it. Dermot had but little natural timidity or shyness; yet he felt somewhat awed when, having missed the back approach used by the servants of the establishment, he found himself at the entrance-hall, in which a number of well-dressed persons were assembled on their way to the breakfast-room. Some passed him carelessly.

"Oh, here, papa, is a fisher-boy with such fine fish," said a young and fair girl as she ran up to a tall and dignified man, who at that moment appeared.

"Why, boy, what brought you here?" asked the gentleman.

"To sell some fish; I caught them myself," was Dermot's answer. "They are fine and fresh. I will not bargain for the price, as I feel sure you will give me what they are worth."

The gentleman seemed amused at the boy's composure, and stepping forward looked into the basket which Dermot opened to exhibit his fish.

"You are right, boy. Send Anderson here," he said, turning to a footman. "We will purchase your fish, and you may come whenever you can bring others as fine."

Several ladies of the party seeing the Earl, for the gentleman who spoke was the owner of the castle, addressing the boy, came forward, and now, for the first time, remarked his handsome features and picturesque, though rough, costume.

The little girl begged that the fish might be taken out of the basket to be shown to her, and seemed delighted with the brightness of their scales and their elegant forms.

"Look after the boy, Anderson, and give him some breakfast," said the Earl, as the head cook appeared, and Dermot, finding himself more noticed than he was ever before in his life, was conducted down below to the servants' quarters. Although they were town servants, and would certainly have disdained to speak to a mere beggar-boy, or to a young country clown, there was something in Dermot's unaffected manner and appearance which won their regard, and they treated him with far more kindness and attention than would otherwise have been the case.

Highly delighted with this his first visit to the castle, Dermot returned to his mother's hut to give

DERMOT, THE FISHER-BOY, AS A MODEL.

her an account of what had occurred. That evening she was sufficiently recovered to accompany him on their usual fishing expedition. Again they were successful, and the next morning Dermot once more made his appearance at the castle. He was received much in the same manner as on the previous occasion. His fish were exhibited before being taken below, and greatly to his astonishment a lady of the party begged that he would stand where he was, with his basket in his hand, while she produced her sketch-book and made a portrait of him. Dermot scarcely understood the process that was going forward, and was somewhat relieved when the breakfast bell sounding, the lady was compelled to abandon her undertaking.

"But I must have you notwithstanding, young fisher-boy," said the lady. "You must come back after breakfast and hold one of those fish in your hand; I have only made the outline, and the drawing will not be perfect until it is well coloured."

"He does not understand the honour that has been done him," observed an elderly dame to the fair artist; "still he looks intelligent, and perhaps when he sees himself on paper he will be better pleased than he appears to be at present."

Dermot scarcely understood all that was said,

for though he spoke English very fairly, he could not comprehend the language when spoken rapidly.

Breakfast being concluded, he was again summoned to the hall, and to his utter astonishment he was made to stand with the fish in his hand, while the young lady continued her sketch. As a reward she exhibited it to him when it was finished. He blushed when he saw himself, for she was no mean artist, and she had done him ample justice. Indeed he looked far more like the Earl's son dressed in a fisher-boy's costume, than what he really was.

"Could my mother see that picture?" he asked at length, "I am sure she would like it, she knows more about those things than I do, for I have never seen anything of that sort before."

"What! Have you never seen a picture before?" exclaimed the young lady in surprise, "nor a print, nor a painting?"

Dermot shook his head—"No, nothing of the sort. I did not think that anything so like life could be put on paper."

"Cannot you read?" asked the lady.

"No," said Dermot, "I have no book. The priest can read, but there are few people else in this part of the country who can do so."

"Oh! you must be taught to read, then," exclaimed the young lady. "It is a pity that you should be so ignorant. Would you not like to learn?" ·

"Yes!" said the boy, looking up, "and to draw such figures as that. I should like to learn to place you on paper. You would make a far more beautiful picture than that is."

The young lady smiled at the boy's unsophisticated compliment: "Well, if you will come to the castle, I will try to teach you to read at all events," she answered. "I should like such a pupil, for I am sure you would learn rapidly."

"And I must help you, Lady Sophy," said the little girl, who had been the first to draw attention to Dermot. "I am sure I should teach him to read very quickly, should I not, little fisher-boy? You would like to learn of me, would you not?"

"Indeed I would," answered Dermot, looking at her with an expression of gratitude. "You are very gentle and kind, but I would not learn of those who try to force me."

"When will you begin?" asked Lady Sophy.

"To-morrow. I long to gain the art you speak of," answered the boy eagerly. "The priest tells me many things I have not known. Perhaps I shall be able to tell him some things he does not know."

"So you wish to show this portrait to your mother?" observed Lady Sophy, in a kind tone. "I cannot trust you with it, but if you will tell me her name and where she lives, we will ride over some day and pay her a visit."

"My mother is Ellen O'Neil, the Widow O'Neil, she is generally called, for my father is dead. She is a kind mother to me, and there are not many like her," answered the boy with a proud tone, showing how highly he prized his remaining parent. "But our hut is not fit for such noble ladies as you are to enter," he added, now gazing round the hall and for the first time comparing it with his own humble abode. "It is but a fisherman's hut, and my mother and I live there alone. You could scarcely indeed ride down to it without the risk of your horses falling. If you will let me have the picture I will promise you faithfully that I will bring it back."

"No, no!" answered the young lady, laughing; 'perhaps your mother might keep it, and I want to nave an excuse for paying her a visit. So we will come, tell her, and we shall not mind how small the hut may be."

Dermot was at length compelled to explain where his mother's hut was to be found, though he again warned the ladies that the approach to it was dangerous, and entreated them to keep well to the right away from the sea as they crossed the downs.

They promised to follow his injunction, and at length allowed him to take his departure. This he was anxious to do, as he knew that it was time to put off, to haul the nets which had been laid down in the morning.

Day after day, while the fine weather lasted and fish were to be procured, Dermot paid a visit to the castle, and each morning after breakfast was over, the young ladies insisted on giving him his reading lesson. He made rapid progress, and after a few days, they gave him a book that he might take home and study by himself.

Hitherto Lady Sophy and her friends at the castle, had not paid their promised visit to the fisherman's cottage. At length, however, one evening just as Dermot and his mother had landed, they heard voices on the downs above their hut, and looking up Dermot espied the party from the castle. They were standing irresolute what path to take. He instantly climbed up the cliff by a pathway which speedily placed him by their side. He begged them to dismount, and undertook to conduct Lady Sophy and the little girl, whom he heard addressed as Lady Nora, down to the hut.

"I have brought the drawing as I promised," said

Lady Sophy, taking a portfolio from the groom who held their horses. "I will show it to your mother, and perhaps she will let me take hers also."

There were other ladies and several gentlemen, and they expressed an intention of coming also down to the hut. Lady Sophy guessed that this would not be pleasant to the boy's mother, and begged them to continue their ride along the downs, promising in a short time to rejoin them. Dermot was greatly relieved, for he knew his mother would be much annoyed at having so many visitors; at the same time he felt equally sure she would be pleased at seeing the two young ladies.

Widow O'Neil had just reached her hut with a basket of fish on her shoulders. As the young ladies entered, conducted by Dermot, she placed two three-legged stools and begged them to be seated, for there was no chair in the hut.

"You have come to honour an old fish-wife with a visit, ladies," she said; "you are welcome. If I l'ved in a palace you would be more welcome still. My boy has told me of your kindness to him. A mother's heart is grateful. I can give nothing in return, but again I say, you are welcome."

"We came to show you a drawing I made of him," said Lady Sophy. "Here, see, do you think it like him?"

"Oh! like him!" exclaimed the widow, lifting up her hands; "indeed, like him, and far more like him who has gone—his father—whose grave lies off there in the cold dark sea. I would that I could possess that drawing, I should prize it more than pearls!"

"I will make you a copy," said Lady Sophy, "on one condition, that you allow me to make a drawing of yourself."

"Of me! of the old fish-wife?" exclaimed the astonished widow. "There is little that would repay you for doing that, lady!"

The young lady smiled as she gazed at the picturesque costume and the still handsome features of the woman, although the signs of age had already come upon them. Her eyes were usually bright, but her cheek and mouth had fallen in, and her figure having lost all the roundness of youth, was thin and wiry.

"Oh yes, you would make a beautiful picture," exclaimed the young lady, looking at her with the enthusiasm of an artist. "Do sit still on that cask for a time with a basket of fish at your feet. You must let me draw you thus. Remember, if you will not, I cannot promise to make a copy of your son's likeness for you."

"As you will, ladies," answered the fish-wife.

"The bribe you offer is great. As for me, it matters little what you make of me. You are likely to give me qualities I do not possess."

Although she used appropriate terms, she spoke the English with some difficulty. It was unusual for any of the peasantry of that part of the coast in those days to speak English, and how she had acquired a knowledge of the language, and had been able to impart it to her son, it was difficult to say. Perhaps her husband might have spoken it, or her younger days might have been passed in some distant part of the country, and yet she had the characteristic features of the people in the south-west of Ireland, many of whom are descended from Spanish settlers, who had crossed over in ancient days from the coast of Spain.

Dermot stood by Lady Nora's side, watching with looks of astonishment the progress made by Lady Sophy's pencil. He hastened to bring her a cup of water that she asked for, to moisten her colours; still greater was his surprise when he saw the tints thrown in and gradually a very perfect portrait produced of his mother.

He clapped his hands with delight. "It's her, it's her," he exclaimed; "I wish that thus she could always be. Oh, lady, if you give my mother a likeness of me, I must ask you to give me a copy of that portrait. It's beautiful; it's like her in every respect. If I were away from her, I should think it could speak to me."

"Away from her," said the woman, looking up and speaking to herself. "Oh, that so dark a day should ever arrive, and yet am I to keep him always by me, perhaps to share the fate of his father."

The words scarcely reached the ears of those in the hut.

At length Dermot obtained a promise from Lady Sophy that she would give him a copy of the portrait she had just taken. He now accompanied her and her young companion to the spot where they had left their horses.

"You must promise to come to-morrow, Dermot," said the Lady Sophy; " we wish to push you on with your lessons, for we shall not be here much longer, and we probably shall not return until next year."

CHAPTER II.

DERMOT promised Lady Sophy to read all the books she had given him. When they left his mother's hut he begged leave to accompany her and Lady Nora, in order that he might see them across the downs. He had discovered during his visits to the castle that the young Lady Nora was the Earl of Kilfinnan's only daughter. He had a son also; a noble little boy he had heard. He was away at school in England; his father being fully conscious that an Irish castle in those days was not a place favourable to education. The Earl had a great affection for his boy, the heir to his title and estates. The former, indeed, should the young Lord Fitz Barry die without male descendants, would pass away, though the Lady Nora would inherit the chief part of his estate.

Lady Sophy was a relation of his late wife's, for he was a widower, and she remained with him as a companion to his young daughter, though considerably older than she was. The rest of the persons seen at the castle were guests, with the exception of a lady of middle age, a Mrs. Rollings, who acted as governess and chaperone to the young ladies.

Dermot continued his visits to the castle. Sometimes the Earl saw him, and seemed amused at the interest taken in him by his young niece and daughter. He observed also, that the boy was somewhat out of the common way, and he suggested that after they had left the west of Ireland, he should be sent to obtain instruction from a neighbouring clergyman, a friend of his, and the only person capable of imparting it.

At that time schools and missions were not known in the west of Ireland. The priests, almost as ignorant as their flocks, had unbounded sway among the population. Often the Protestant clergyman was the only person for miles round who possessed any education whatever. The peasantry were consequently ignorant and superstitious and easily imposed upon by any one who chose to go among them with that object.

Lady Sophy was delighted with the suggestion made by the Earl, and insisted on at once carrying out the arrangement.

"Yes, indeed it is a pity that so intelligent a boy should be left in ignorance," remarked the Earl. "Here is a five-pound note; do you take it from me to Mr. Jamieson, and beg that he will do his best to instil some knowledge into the mind of the fisher-boy."

There was a dash of romance, it must be owned, in the Earl's composition, and he was besides a kind-hearted and liberal man. Dermot O'Neil might well have considered himself fortunate in having fallen among such friends.

Lady Sophy and Lady Nora instantly set off to call upon Mr. Jamieson, whose vicarage was about three miles distant from the castle, though somewhat nearer to Dermot's abode. The clergyman was rather amused at first with the account given him by the young ladies. He promised, however, to follow out the Earl's wishes, and begged that Dermot might come to him directly they left the country; "And I shall be ready to undertake his education at once, Lady Sophy," he said.

"No, no!" was the answer; "we cannot give him up yet; it is quite a pleasure teaching him. He already reads English with tolerable fluency, though we have not attempted yet to teach him to write. We must leave that to you."

Dermot, with a grief he had not expected to feel, saw the party take their departure from the castle. The young ladies kindly nodded to him as their carriage rolled past the spot where he stood.

"There's a bright light gone from amongst us," he said to himself. "Did I ever before dream that such creatures existed on earth."

He returned to his home in a mood totally strange to him. His mother, however, had reason to congratulate herself on the Earl's visit, for it enabled her, from the payment she received for her fish, to provide in a way she had never before done for the coming winter. This made her the more willingly consent that Dermot should go over every day to obtain instruction from Mr. Jamieson, the good clergyman, who was so pleased with the fisher-boy, that he took particular pains in instructing him, and not only was Dermot in a short time able to read any book that was put into his hands, but he also learned to write with considerable ease. His mind naturally expanded with the books given him to study, and as he obtained information, he became greedy for more.

Although Mr. Jamieson had at first only intended teaching him the simple rudiments of reading and writing, he became so interested in the progress made by his pupil, that he felt desirous of imparting all the knowledge Dermot was capable of acquiring.

Thus the winter passed away. Dermot, in spite of wind and rain, or sleet or cold, persevered in his visits to the vicarage. He gained also an acquaintance with religious truth, of which before he had been profoundly ignorant. It was not very perfect, perhaps, but Mr. Jamieson put the Bible into his hands, and he thus obtained a knowledge of its contents possessed by few of those around. Had the neighbouring parish priest, Father O'Rourke, discovered whither he was going, and the change that was constantly taking place in him, he would probably have endeavoured to interfere, and prevent him from paying his visits to the Protestant clergyman. Although he might not have hindered Dermot from doing as he chose, he probably would have alarmed his mother, who, though tolerably intelligent was too completely under the influence of superstition to have understood clearly the cause of the priest's interference. In a certain sense, to Dermot's mind, the advantage he possessed was not so great as at first sight might appear. As he advanced in knowledge he became less and less contented with his lot in life, or rather the wish increased that he might be able to raise himself above it. By what means, however, was this to be accomplished? He had no claim upon the Earl, who, although wishing that he might be taught reading and writing, had not the slightest intention of raising him above his present occupation. Mr.

Jamieson gave him no encouragement; although perhaps, the idea had occurred to the worthy minister, that the boy was fitted for something above the mere life of an ordinary fisherman. Still the matter had not as yet troubled Dermot's mind. It probably only occasionally passed through his thoughts, that there was an existence, even in this world something above that to which it appeared he was doomed. Mr. Jamieson had now resided for a considerable number of years at the vicarage. He came there with high anticipations of the amount of good he was likely to effect in that neighbourhood. By degrees, however, he found that his efforts to raise the people out of the state of ignorance in which they had been brought up were likely to prove abortive. The parish priest did not indeed offer him any open opposition, but he set an under current to work, which silently, though effectually nullified all the vicar's efforts. Not one proselyte had he made, and at length he abandoned his previous intentions in despair of success, and consoled himself with the thought that at least he would perform thoroughly all the duties of his station. To such a conclusion many persons in his position have arrived, whether rightly or wrongly it need not here be said. Mr. Jamieson had an only niece, who had of late years come to reside with him. She was no longer very young but was a gentle, quiet woman, whose great desire was to do any good to her fellow-creatures which lay in her power.

Miss O'Reilly had been for some time aware that a severe affliction was about to overtake her. When she first arrived at the vicarage, she used to go among the neighbouring peasantry, carrying a basket to relieve the sick or starving, or to administer such comfort as she was able. She enjoyed the beautiful scenery by which she was surrounded. Now, however, she found that when she took a book the letters were dim and indistinct, while all distant scenes were shut out from her view, as if a thick mist hung over them. Blindness she felt was coming on. A journey to Dublin was in those days a long and tedious, if not somewhat dangerous undertaking. Still, at her uncle's desire, accompanied by him, she performed it. But no hope was given by the oculist whom she consulted, and she returned home with the knowledge that in a short time she would require some one to lead her by the hand whenever she might wish to move from the immediate neighbourhood of the house.

Dermot had made frequent visits to the vicarage before Miss O'Reilly was aware who he was. One day he met her while she was trying to find her way a short distance from the house. He had seen her and knew who she was. Seeing her in doubt as to the path she was to take, he, with the native gallantry of the Irish, sprang forward and begged that he might be allowed to lead her.

"And who are you, boy?" she asked. "What brings you to the vicarage?"

Dermot told her his short history.

"You are then a pupil of my uncle's?"

"Yes, his reverence has been teaching me, and I love to learn from him," answered Dermot.

This led to further conversation, and Dermot told her of his mother, who lived down in the little cottage in Blackwater cove.

"And have you any brothers, sisters, or relations?" she asked.

"Except Uncle Shane, none that I know of," said Dermot.

"Your mother, then, lives all alone."

"Yes, since my father's death, twelve years ago, she has lived by herself, with me alone to take care of, in her little hut."

"And you never wish to leave your home, and go and see the great world?" asked Miss O'Reilly. Why she put the question it was difficult to say. It might not have been a very judicious one, as far as the boy was concerned, and yet it was but natural to suppose that a boy of Dermot's character would wish to go forth into the great world, that he might inspect its wonders.

"It may be, lady; I may have wished to go and see the world, though not to leave my mother; for who would care for her if I was gone? Uncle Shane would, but he is old and couldn't protect her for long. Besides you know that not a year passes but that some of the men on our coast lose their lives."

"And does your mother know the truth? Can she read the Bible, boy?" asked Miss O'Reilly.

"No, she cannot read the Bible, but the priest takes care that she should know what he believes to be the truth, I am sure.".

"Your mother loves you?"

"Oh! indeed she does," answered Dermot; "she would spill her heart's blood for my sake, though she often sits melancholy and sad when alone, yet the moment I return, her eye brightens, and she opens her arms to receive me. Yes, lady, my mother does love me, that I know."

"I should like to come and talk to your mother," said the blind lady. "Will you lead me to her some day? I should not be afraid to descend the cliff with so strong an arm as yours to rest on."

A few days after this, Dermot having finished his

lesson with the vicar, met Miss O'Reilly close to the house, and expressed his readiness to take her to his mother's cottage, the sea at the time happening to be far too rough to allow their boat to go forth to fish.

"I am ready to go with you," said the blind lady; "but remember you must lead me all the way back, Dermot."

"That will just double the honour, lady," was the young Irishman's reply. Dermot talked much of his mother to the blind lady, as he led her down to the cottage.

The widow's voice pleased Miss O'Reilly, and all she said increased the interest she was inclined to take in her. Perhaps more than all, was that deep love which she felt for her only boy, and which had become, as it were, part of her being.

Dermot carefully conducted Miss O'Reilly back to the vicarage, and this was the first of many visits which she afterwards paid to the fish-wife's hut.

Dermot was never idle. He had no associates; indeed from his earliest days he had kept aloof from boys of his own age. It was not that he was morose, or proud or ill-tempered, but he appeared to have no sympathy with them, and thus, though possessed of many qualities which would have won him friends, he had not a single friend of his own rank or age in the neighbourhood. Whenever he was not out fishing, he was engaged with his book, either at the vicarage or at home.

He was thus employed one afternoon in his mother's hut, when Father O'Rourke, the parish priest, made his appearance at the door.

"Come in, your reverence," said the widow, placing a stool for him near the hearth; "it is a long day since your reverence has been seen down the cove."

"Maybe you haven't seen me often enough," said Father O'Rourke, a stout broad-faced man, with a countenance of the ordinary low Irish type. "How is it that Dermot there has so many books? Ah! I have heard about his doings; he often goes up, I am told, to the Protestant minister's. What good can he get by going there?"

"Much good, your reverence," observed Dermot; "I have been learning to read and write, and gain other knowledge such as I had no other means of obtaining."

"Such knowledge may be bad for one like you," said Father O'Rourke; "there is no good can come from the place where you go to get it."

"Pardon me, Father O'Rourke," said Dermot, with spirit; "the knowledge I get there is good, and the gentleman who gives it is kind and good too. I will not hear him spoken against."

"What, lad! do you dare to speak to me in that way?" exclaimed the priest. "You will be going over to the Protestants, and then the curse of St. Patrick and all the holy saints will rest upon you,—you too, who are born to be a priest of the holy faith. Look; you were marked before you came into the world with the emblem of our faith, and if your mother had followed the wishes of her true friends, you would even now be training for the priesthood, instead of being a poor fisher-boy, as you now must be for ever, and nothing more." The priest as he spoke seized Dermot's hand, and bared his arm to the shoulder. There, curiously enough, above the elbow, was a red mark which might easily have been defined as a cross.

The boy drew away his hand indignantly: "I tell you, Father O'Rourke, I am as true a son of the Holy Church as ever I was. Mr. Jamieson is no bigot; he gives me instruction, but does not ask me to turn to his faith, and yet, Father O'Rourke, I tell you, to my mind it is a pure and holy faith, whatever you may say to the contrary."

The boy spoke boldly and proudly, as he again drew down the sleeve of his shirt.

Many years before, when the red mark on Dermot's arm had first been seen by the neighbours, it was suggested that it was evidently placed there as a sign from heaven that he should become a priest, and that in all probability he would rise to be a bishop, if not a cardinal. When, however, Dermot grew a little older, and the idea was suggested to him, he indignantly refused to accept the offers made him. In the first place, nothing would induce him to leave his mother, and in the second, he had no ambition to become like Father O'Rourke, for whom it must be confessed, that at a very early age the boy had entertained a considerable antipathy. Even with the widow, though she was ignorant and superstitious, Father O'Rourke had never been a favourite; still when she could get so far as the chapel, she went to hear mass, and attended confession, as did her neighbours. The feeling which governed her was fear, rather than love for the parish priest. Father O'Rourke was excessively indignant at being thus addressed by the young fisher-boy. He turned from him, however, to his mother, and began to pour out his abuse on her head. He had not proceeded far, however, when Dermot again sprang to his feet.

"Father O'Rourke!" he exclaimed; "you may say what you like to me; you may curse me, and if you like you may threaten me with excommunication even, but do not lift up your tongue against my poor old mother. There are things a man can bear and some he ought not to bear, and I tell you, boy as I am, I will not have her spoken against. Your words may frighten her, and she may fancy that your curses may fall upon her head, but I tell you when uttered against a poor helpless widow, they will fall back on him who dares to speak them. There, Father O'Rourke, I have had my say, and I defy you."

The priest had never before been spoken to in this manner by one of his flock, and he found no words to reply. At first he felt inclined to anathematise both the widow and her son, but doubts as to the effects it might produce upon Dermot restrained him, or perhaps a better feeling came into his heart.

"Very well, boy, remember I have warned you," he exclaimed, "I have told you that by going to that Protestant minister, you may be led to turn heretic, and forsake our holy faith, and if you should, do not forget the heavy curses that will follow you. I do not wish you ill, nor do I wish your mother ill, but I cannot stand by and see one of my flock carried the downward way to destruction."

Having thus delivered himself, Father O'Rourke

left the hut and took the path up the steep glen, which led inland from the sea.

Often Dermot's mind reverted to the days when the castle was inhabited, and he thought of the beautiful and kind ladies he had seen there, and of the fair little girl who had smiled so sweetly when she spoke to him. He felt the immeasurable distance between them and him, and yet he longed for their return, that he might gaze on them at a distance, and again hear their voices. He was generally too much occupied to go to the castle to inquire when the Earl was likely to return, because when not engaged in fishing, he was constantly at the house of Mr. Jamieson. More than once he had ventured to ask him whether he thought the Earl was likely to come back again, but the minister replied that he was ignorant of the Earl's movements, and had not heard that any orders had been received at the castle to make preparations for the reception of the family. The time was approaching when they had come on the previous year, and Dermot though he scarcely acknowledged his feelings to himself, became more and more anxious for their arrival. After leaving Mr. Jamieson, though the round was a long one, and he had to prepare his nets for the day's fishing, he could not resist the temptation of going to the castle before he returned home. From his frequent visits during the previous summer, he was not a stranger there, and the housekeeper, pleased with his good looks and his unaffected manner, was not sorry to see him.

"Wait a bit, boy, wait a bit, and I think I can tell you when the ladies will come back and make another likeness of you," she said, putting her hand on his head. "Ah! they will spoil you if we don't take care, but do not be led away by them, boy. They look upon you, likely enough, as they do upon a pet dog, or any other animal, and when they are away, it is little they trouble their heads about you."

These remarks were made in kindness by good Mrs. Rafferty. She had heard all about the boy, and knew very well that if it became the custom to have him up at the castle, and to make much of him, as she thought was likely to be the case, he would inevitably be spoiled.

"When you come we will buy your fish, no fear of that, and take my advice, get a supply of the finest you can by to-morrow or the day after, and maybe when you come there will be mouths enough at the castle to eat them."

"What! are the family coming so soon then?" exclaimed Dermot, and a thrill of pleasure ran through his frame; "and the beautiful lady who draws so well, and all the others! I will go and catch the fish, never fear, Mrs. Rafferty, and it will not be my fault if I don't bring a basket of as fine as ever were caught up to the castle to-morrow."

"I did not say 'to-morrow,' boy; I said the day after, and that will be time enough."

Mrs. Rafferty, to prove her kind feelings, took the boy into her own room, and placed before him several articles of food and delicacies, such as had never before passed his lips. She watched him while he ate.

"It is strange if there's not gentle blood in that boy," she remarked to herself, "I have heard what the young ladies think about it, and by the way he sits at table and eats I never would believe that he is a mere fisher-boy."

Dermot did not hear her remarks. Having finished his repast, he rose and wishing her good-bye, hastened home with the good news to his mother.

CHAPTER III.

THE widow and her son devoted the next day to an active supervision of their nets. In the evening a gentle westerly breeze, which had brought in their boat safely to shore, was still blowing, and Dermot having prepared the fish for the next day's market, ascended to the downs above the cottage. As he gazed over the ocean, he saw under all sail, standing in for the shore, a beautiful ship. She had royals set, and studding sails below and aloft on either side. It was evident she wished to come to an anchor before dark, and he concluded from the course she was steering, that she proposed bringing up in the bay, a reef extending out, on the north side of it, affording her sufficient shelter from the wind then blowing. Dermot watched the ship with intense interest. The masts seemed so tall, the canvas so white, and the yards extending so far on either side. On she came like a graceful swan, gliding over the azure bosom of the deep, surrounded as it were with the golden rays of the setting sun playing over the water in which she floated. Dermot had not believed that any vessel so beautiful was to be found on the ocean. She seemed so graceful, so fairy-like. As she drew nearer her sides appeared highly polished, and all about her wore an air of perfect order. A distant strain of music reached his ear from the deck. On a sudden men were seen swarming up her rigging. Every yard was covered. Now the studding sails came in as if by magic. The royals and the topgallant sails were handed, the topsails were furled, the courses brailed up, and in a few seconds she was under bare poles, when her anchor was let go with a loud rattling sound in the securest part of the bay, showing that those on board were well acquainted with the coast.

As he looked down on the gallant frigate, for such she was, Dermot's admiration increased more and more. He could not help wishing to be on board so fine a craft, and he determined to take the first opportunity of visiting her.

On his return to the hut, he told his mother of the arrival of the frigate.

"She comes as a friend, I hope," remarked the widow; "it is not many years ago that I have seen vessels in this bay, which came with very different intentions."

No one was seen, however, to land from the strange frigate, but the widow, on further consideration, resolved to pay a visit on board, in hopes of disposing of the fish they had just caught, calculating that a further supply might be obtained for the castle the following day.

Dermot was glad of an excuse for going on board: as it was now too late to visit her, it was arranged that they should go off the first thing on the following morning. Although he and his mother could manage the boat by themselves, he did not know how she might be received on board; he therefore invited his Uncle Shane to accompany them, advising him to carry a supply of his own fish for sale.

Early the next morning the boat was alongside the frigate. The vendors of fish are generally welcomed by men-of-war's-men, and they very quickly disposed of all they possessed; the only complaint of the sailors being, that they had not brought off enough vegetables and other fresh productions.

Dermot was invited on board, and as he showed his curiosity in all he saw, he was allowed to go over the whole of the ship. Great was his wonder as he examined her polished guns, the decks, white as snow, one below the other, the ropes on the upper deck so beautifully flemished down. The men were at breakfast, between decks. The tin mess untensils were spread out before them. Dermot was shown how the hammocks were hung up at night, and where they were stowed in the hammock nettings in the daytime. He gazed aloft at the symmetrical yards and ropes, and wondered at the perfect order which reigned around; so different to what he had been accustomed to in the small fishing-vessels and coasters, the only craft with which he was acquainted.

"Would you like to come to sea, lad?" said a rough sailor, putting his hand on Dermot's shoulder; "you would make an active young topman in a few years. There's something in you, I see. What do you say? Will you ship aboard us? I can answer for it you would get a berth, for our captain likes such as you."

Dermot was pleased with the compliment paid him, though uttered in a rough way.

"Ah! if I had my heart's wish, I would do as you say," he answered; "but there's one I cannot leave, and I do not think you would if you were in my place."

"Who's that?" asked the sailor.

"My mother, I am her only child," answered Dermot.

"I ran away from my mother, and yet I was her only son," replied the sailor, as he dashed a tear from his eye. "No, boy, I am not one to advise you to do as I did. I know not whether she is alive or dead, for never from that day to this have I had the chance of returning home."

The widow was highly pleased with the transactions on board, for whatever spice of romance there was in her, she never forgot the importance of making a good bargain for her fish. Shane was delighted, and undertook to return on board the next day.

Another successful expedition enabled Dermot to carry a supply of fish to Mrs. Rafferty at the castle. His modesty induced him to enter by the back way, and on asking for her, after waiting some time, he was told he might go and see her in her room. The good lady told him that she expected the family every instant, and would take all the fish he had brought. Dermot hurried away, fearful that they might arrive while he was in the castle, and that he might lose the opportunity of seeing them. He sat himself down by the side of the road which the carriages must pass, in the hopes of gaining a glimpse of the lady who had taken his portrait, as well as of the fair little girl her companion. He thought very little of the rest of the party. At length, after waiting some time his patience was rewarded by seeing the carriages approach. Not only were the ladies there, but they both saw him, and Lady Nora gave a half-nod of recognition, and then turned to her companion, as if to speak about him. Dermot would gladly have found any excuse for returning to the castle, but as this was impossible, he hurried home, hoping to be able to visit it the next day with a further supply of fish. On his way he saw a boat pulling rapidly from the frigate towards the landing-place under the castle-walls. In her stern-sheets sat an officer, who by the gold epaulets on his shoulders and his cocked hat, he naturally concluded was the captain. Poor Dermot had very little chance after this of attracting the attention of Lady Sophy. The boat reached the shore, when the captain sprang out, and hurried up to the castle. He was received with great courtesy and respect by the Earl and his guests.

"You are indeed welcome, Falkner!" exclaimed the Earl, cordially shaking him by the hand, "we little expected having the pleasure of seeing you. What fortunate chance brings you into our bay?"

"We received information that there was some idea of a rising in this part of the country, and I was ordered to cruise off the coast," answered the captain of the frigate. "Hearing also that you were about to return to Kilfinnan Castle, as it was in the way of duty, I took the opportunity of coming into the bay to visit you, and at the same time to make inquiries as to the truth of the report."

"You are very welcome, Captain Falkner, and we are very happy to see you," said the Earl, casting a significant glance towards Lady Sophy; "as to the rising, I rather think the Government has been misled; however, it is as well to be prepared, and the appearance of the frigate on the coast may prevent the people from committing any act of folly."

"I hope so, indeed," said Captain Falkner; "for the blood of too many of the misguided people has been shed already. They may bring much misery and suffering on themselves, and they may do a great deal of mischief in the country, but while England's fleet- and England's army remain faithful, their wild schemes have not the remotest prospect of success."

"No, indeed!" answered the Earl, in a somewhat scornful tone, "unless men of character and true bravery were to lead them, they will always be defeated as they have hitherto been. For my own part I have not the slightest fear on the subject. However, I repeat that I am not sorry that any excuse should have brought you into our bay."

Captain Falkner after this received the welcome

of the rest of the guests, with most of whom he was acquainted.

Lady Sophy blushed as she held out her hand, and the gallant captain took it with a look which showed there was a perfect understanding between them. He had already obtained a name which gave him rank among the bravest of England's naval heroes. They before long found an excuse for walking out together on a beautiful terrace, which extended under the cliffs, beyond the castle to the south. The conversation need not be repeated, it was very evident, however, that Captain Falkner was an accepted suitor of Lady Sophy's, although there were some impediments to their immediate union.

He told her that he expected to be on the coast for some time, for he still believed, in spite of the Earl's assertions, that there was a considerable number of persons disaffected in that part of the country, who would be induced to rise, should a leader make his appearance among them.

"Although I may sail away for a few days at a time, I shall constantly be on the watch, and the thought that you may be placed in danger, will certainly not make me the less vigilant," he observed, pressing Lady Sophy's hand.

"But suppose you were to hear there would be a

rising in this place, and another at some distance, to which would you then go?" asked Lady Sophy. "Would it not place you in a difficulty?"

"I tell you frankly, I would endeavour to forget in which place you were, and should steer for the one in which I believed my services were most imperatively demanded."

"Yes, I am sure you would act thus," she answered, casting on him a look of admiration and affection. "I do not value your love the less on that account, believe me."

Captain Falkner had to return on board in the evening, but promised to visit the castle next day.

He arrived just as Dermot made his appearance with a basket of fish.

"Oh! that is the boy whose portrait you were admiring so much, Captain Falkner," said Lady Sophy, pointing to Dermot as he was passing the hall-door.

"Come in, boy," said another lady; "we wish to see if your portrait has done you justice."

Dermot entered in his usual fearless manner, carrying his basket of fish. The portrait was produced, and another lady insisted that he should remain until she had taken a sketch of him for herself.

"By-the-by," said the Earl, "have you got any good by going to the minister, boy?"

"Yes, indeed I have, sir," said Dermot warmly, "there is many a book I have learned to read, and though I found writing more hard, I am able to copy whatever Mr. Jamieson gives me, and while he reads I can write after him. And there is history and geography and many more things he has taught me."

"Ah, I must go over and thank him," said the Earl. "And do you wish, boy, to continue under his instruction ?"

"Indeed I do, sir," answered Dermot.

"Oh, but we were teaching you," exclaimed Lady Nora, who had just then come into the hall. "You must come and let Lady Sophy and me give you lessons as we did before."

"Indeed I am honoured, ladies," answered Dermot, with an air which none but an Irish boy, even of much higher rank, could have assumed. "Although I am grateful to the minister for all he has taught me, I should be thankful to receive further lessons from you."

The Earl was somewhat amused at the thoughts of his little daughter giving instruction to the young fisher-boy. At the same time, goodnatured and thoughtless, he made not the slightest objection. Indeed he never thwarted Nora in anything she had taken it into her head to wish for, and certainly he was not likely to do so in a matter so trifling as this.

Dermot appeared, as he had been invited, to receive his lessons, but was somewhat surprised to find that Lady Nora was scarcely as advanced in some branches of knowledge as himself.

"Indeed you have made great progress," said Lady Sophy, who had undertaken to be the chief instructress. "If you persevere you will soon become as well educated as most young gentlemen of the day. I am acquainted with several, indeed, who don't know as much as you do."

These remarks encouraged Dermot to persevere, even with more determination than before. Every moment he could spare from his duties, he was now engaged in reading.

His poor mother looked on with astonishment that her boy should thus become so learned, and more than once it entered into her mind that it was a pity she had not allowed him to follow Father O'Rourke's suggestion, and become a priest. "He would have been a bishop to a certainty," she exclaimed to herself—"and only think to be a holy bishop, certain of heaven. What a great man he would have been made, a cardinal, and that he would have been, if His Holiness the Pope had ever become acquainted with him. I wonder now if it's too late, but I'm afraid after what he said to Father O'Rourke that his Reverence will never give him a helping hand."

Such and similar thoughts frequently passed through the mind of the poor widow. More than once she ventured to broach the subject to her son, but he shook his head with a look of disgust.

"If I am ever to be otherwise than what I am, I hope never to become like Father O'Rourke. No, no, mother I have other thoughts, and do not, I pray you, ever ask me again to become a priest."

The next visit Dermot paid to the castle, he was detained longer than usual by another lady insisting on taking his portrait. His feelings rather rebelled against this. He had been flattered when Lady Sophy had first taken it, but he did not much like the idea of being made a figure for the exercise of other fair artists' pencils, still his natural feelings of politeness prevented him from showing the annoyance he felt.

While the lady was proceeding with her work, he gathered from the conversation around him that some one of importance was expected at the castle, and he at length made out that the young heir—Lord Fitz Barry—was looked for during the afternoon.

Dermot had never seen him, for during the previous summer, he had not returned home, having remained with his tutor in England. He found that the carriage had been sent for the young Lord to the neighbouring town.

As soon as the ladies dismissed him, Dermot took his way along the road by which he would reach the castle.

He had not long to wait before he saw an open carriage with the Earl in it, and by his side a young boy bearing a strong resemblance to Lady Nora.

There were the same blue eyes and the fair complexion and rich auburn air possessed by his sister, at the same time there was a manly look and expression in his countenance—boy as he was—which at once won Dermot's respect.

"Ah, he has the old blood of his family in his veins," thought Dermot, "and when he comes to man's estate he'll prove, I hope, the same kind-hearted, honest man that his father is."

Well pleased with his morning visit to the castle, Dermot returned to his humble cottage. Did he ever draw a contrast between the two abodes? Yes, but he was not discontented with his lot. He loved his mother, and he knew that his mother loved him above all earthly things, and that she would not exchange him, even to dwell in that lordly castle. Still, as Dermot advanced in knowledge and in age, he could not help discovering that his mother was ignorant and prone to superstition. Indeed with pain he sometimes suspected that her mind was not altogether perfectly right. She would sit occasionally talking to herself, and now and then speak of strange events which had passed in her youth, of which she would give no explanation. He, however, quickly banished this latter idea, as too painful to be entertained. She loved him, what more could he desire? When he was anxious about her, he reflected that she had secured more than one friend in the neighbourhood. That his uncle Shane was devoted to her, and that the kind Miss O'Reilly had promised always to watch over her.

Many wild thoughts and schemes passed frequently through Dermot's mind. He dared not at first give utterance to them, not even to himself, and he would have found it impossible to mention them to any human being.

Mr. Jamieson, more than once, had spoken to him of the future, and hinted that if the way was open to him, he would scarcely fail, with the talents and application he possessed, of rising in life. It was very natural in Mr. Jamieson to think this, for he knew that a fisher-boy's existence on the west coast of Ireland was one of ill-requited toil, and of great danger. Holding this opinion, he felt that the boy would not change for the worse, and would certainly improve his position in whatever calling he might engage.

CHAPTER IV.

ONE afternoon, when it was blowing too hard to allow Dermot to put to sea in his boat, he had gone to the vicarage to obtain his usual instruction, carrying with him some fish he had caught, as a present to the vicar's niece. After he had received his instruction and was about to take his departure, Miss O'Reilly called him back to thank him for the fish which he had brought her.

"By-the-by!" observed Mr. Jamieson, "Dermot can take the pony which I wish to send for young Lord Fitz Barry, and the cloak which he left here the other day."

Dermot had not often ridden; but where is the Irish boy who would not undertake to mount the most fiery steed if he was asked to do so?

He gladly promised to take the pony and cloak to the castle. It was already late in the day, but he observed that "that did not matter," as it must be a dark night in which he could not find his way home. The pony was, however, in the field, and some more time elapsed before he was caught. Miss O'Reilly then bethought her, that Dermot had been a long time without food, and insisted on his taking some before he set off on that blustering evening. It was thus almost dark before he left the vicarage for the castle. He looked down on the bay: the frigate still lay at anchor there, the wind being still from the north.

"If the wind shifts a little more to the west, she will have to put to sea," thought Dermot. "It will not do for her to remain in the bay with the wind blowing in from the west, and with such a sea as often rolls in here, enough to cast the stoutest ship high upon the beach, or to dash her to fragments should she touch the rocks."

Dermot rode on, not, however, very fast, as the little animal was unwilling to leave his own home, not guessing the comfortable quarters to which he was bound. The wind brought up a heavy shower of rain and hail; Dermot was doubtful whether he ought to shelter himself under the young lord's cloak. "Still," he thought, "it will not be the worse for being on my shoulders, and I shall be wet through and well-nigh frozen before I reach the castle, if I am to sit on this animal's back exposed to the storm."

He wisely therefore, having overcome his scruples, put on the cloak, and continued his course as fast as the pony would condescend to go towards the castle.

Just as the frigate was hid from his view by some intervening downs, he thought he saw the men going aloft to loose the topsails, an indication of the ship being about to get under weigh.

"It is the wisest thing that can be done," he thought to himself. "She can easily stand off until the summer gale is over, and run no risk of being driven on shore."

He was already at no great distance from the castle, when suddenly from behind some rocks and bushes which lay near the road, a number of men sprang up and seized the bridle of his pony. He was too much astonished to cry out, or to ask what was their purpose in thus attacking him.

By the expressions that they uttered, however, he soon discovered that they were under the impression that they had got possession of the young lord.

"Now," he thought to himself, with admirable presence of mind, "the best thing I can do is to hold my tongue, and just see what they intended to do with him. I would a great deal rather that they caught hold of me, to whom it matters not what harm they do, than the young lord. I would willingly save him for his sweet sister's sake, and for his too, for he is a kind boy, with a gentle heart. I am sure of that. There is no pride or haughtiness about him. If there were, I should not feel disposed to serve him. No, I could not do that. Well, I will see what these men want to do with him. They will be rather surprised and enraged maybe when they find whom they have got, instead of the young lord."

These thoughts passed rapidly through Dermot's mind, as he saw that he was surrounded by an armed band of men. They did not attempt to pull him from his pony, but turning round the animal's head, they led him across the country inland at a rapid rate, a man holding the rein on either side with a firm grasp, to prevent the little animal from falling over the rough ground they were traversing.

Dermot firmly kept to his resolution of saying nothing. The night was so dark, that had it not been for his knowledge of the direction from which the wind blew, he would have been unable to guess where he was going. In a short time, however, he found the wind blew directly in his teeth. He knew that they must be travelling north, and also, from the character of the ground, that they had already passed beyond the vicarage, and that they could be at no great distance from his own home. Now they turned once more to the west, and he felt sure they were approaching the sea. The ground became more and more wild and rugged, and he guessed by feeling that they continued to ascend for some distance, that they had reached a range of wild hills which lay in that direction.

All this time he had keep his senses wide awake, nor did he allow himself to feel the slightest fear of what was likely to happen.

"No great harm can come to me," at length he thought to himself; "and if it does, what matters it? There are those who will look after my mother, and I shall have saved the young lord from some plot which these ruffians have formed against him."

All this time the people round him were speaking the native Irish, little supposing that their prisoner understood every word they said. He was at length able to gather from their conversation that they intended to hold the young lord as a hostage, threatening, if the demands they proposed making were not granted, that they would kill him in revenge.

At length, he was ordered to dismount, and he found himself led forward through a narrow passage, with rocks on either side, which conducted them into the interior of a cave. It was of considerable size, the roof and sides covered apparently with smoke, probably the result of the illicit distillery which existed, or had existed there. It was dimly lighted by a lamp fixed on a projecting point of the rock. This enabled Dermot to see that a number of arms were piled up along one side, muskets, pikes, and swords. There were two small field-pieces, and what he supposed to be cases of ammunition. Had the light been greater he would probably have been at once discovered. As it was, however, he was led forthwith to the farther part of the cave, where he was told to take a seat on a rough bed-place.

"We'll be after bringing your food directly," said a man, the first person who had spoken to him since his capture. "You will be quiet now, and not attempt to run away; for we should shoot you if you did without the slightest ceremony. You understand that? Or stay, if we were to bind one of your feet to the leg of this bunk, we should have you more secure, I'm thinking."

Dermot, adhering to his resolution, said nothing in return, but allowed himself to be secured as the man proposed. He laughed, however, to himself at the thought of the ease with which he could immediately liberate himself should he wish to do so, and wrapping himself closely in the cloak, the better to conceal his figure and dress, should by chance a gleam of light fall upon him, he lay down on the bunk.

Other persons now continued to arrive, until the cave was full of men, the greater part of whom were peasants or small farmers; at least their comrades treated them with but little ceremony,

As Dermot, however, was watching what took place, he heard the men whispering to each other, "It's him! It's him; he's come to lead us, no fear now."

Just then a man appeared at the entrance of the cave. As he advanced with a confident, indeed somewhat swaggering step, towards the table in the centre, all the men rose from their seats and greeted him in various tones of welcome.

He told them that he had been narrowly watched, that he had had no little difficulty in escaping his enemies and their enemies, that he was thankful to find himself among them, and prepared to undertake any enterprise, however hazardous, which might tend to forward their great and glorious cause—the overthrow of their Saxon tyrants and the establishment of the Irish race as the lords and rulers of their country. He said a great deal more to the same effect, which was eagerly listened to by the assembled rebels.

"Long life to the O'Higgins, he's the boy for

us," resounded through the cavern, or at least words to that effect in the native Irish, the only language spoken by those present.

The O'Higgins spoke it, but Dermot remarked that he did so with some difficulty.

The conspirators seemed highly delighted at having made so valuable a prize, and began in no subdued voices, to discuss their future plans and proceedings.

Dermot listened eagerly, anxious to catch every word that was uttered. He found that they were a band of United Irishmen, as the rebels were generally called at that time, and that in spite of the ill-success of their undertaking in the north, they proposed carrying out a rising in that part of the country. Their first object was to attack the Castle of Kilfinnan, where they hoped to find a supply of arms and a large amount of booty. They expected also to extract a considerable sum for the ransom of the prisoners they might capture in the castle, and, if not, they proposed putting them all to death, in revenge for the execution of their fellow-rebels, which had taken place in other parts of the country.

The chief impediment to their plan was the continuance of the frigate on the coast. They were anxious to devise some plan by which she might be drawn off to another part of Ireland, or induced, at all events, to put to sea. Some of the boldest of the party proposed collecting a flotilla of boats, and taking possession of her, in the belief that they could land her guns and other arms, and thus obtain the means of better competing with the royal troops.

These and many other schemes were freely discussed by the rebels. After some time another person entered the cavern. Dermot looked up and saw by the light of the lamp, which fell on his countenance, that the new comer was no other than Father O'Rourke. He and the O'Higgins greeted each other warmly. It was evident that they were looked upon as the leaders of the undertaking. The one active in a spiritual capacity, urging on the infatuated men the justice of their cause and promising them his own prayers and the protection of Heaven, and telling them to go on and conquer; the other inviting them to follow him, and promising them the victory. Father O'Rourke particularly advocated the most energetic measures. He even advised that they should at once march towards the castle, and, exposing the young lord to view, threaten to hang him if the gates were not opened to admit them.

This plan was, however, overruled by others, who

declared that the frigate still lay in the bay, and that whatever the Earl might do, their appearance on the shore would certainly bring the shot of her guns about their ears.

"And what are you afraid of, comrades?" exclaimed Father O'Rourke. "If they do, cannot I give each of you the blessed picture of St. Patrick, and won't that, worn about your neck, guard you from the shot of the enemy? Ah, if you knew the value of those blessed amulets, you would all of you be anxious to purchase them. No soldier should ever think of going into battle without such a safeguard. Have I not been offering up prayers day and night for the last month for your success, and are you such heretics as to believe that they have all been uttered in vain? No, trust me, let us go and attack the castle this night or to-morrow at farthest, and depend upon it, we shall gain such a victory as will make all the people in the country around rise up and join us. They only want to see a little success, and Ireland shall have her own again. What, boys! are we to be kept down by the red coats, and the vile heretics who call George the Third king? No, I say again. Ireland for the Irish. May St. Patrick and all the blessed Saints fight for us, and we will have true liberty once more in the green Isle of old Erin!"

While listening to the address of the priest, very similar to many others uttered then, and even at the present day, by the so-called pastors of the Romish Church in Ireland, Dermot was thinking over what he should attempt to do. He knew perfectly well from the way his feet had been tied to the bed, that he could liberate himself immediately; but how to steal out of the cavern without being observed was the difficulty; even should the chief body of the rebels go to sleep, it was not likely that they would leave the cavern without a guard. If he could escape, however, he thought his best plan would be to hasten off to the castle, to which he felt sure he could find his way, and give notice of the plans of the conspirators.

"The Earl probably does not dream of an attack being made on his residence, and will not certainly be prepared," thought Dermot to himself. "Perhaps the rebels will steal towards the chief door and break it open before any one within can stop them. The frigate, too, if she has not sailed already, will very likely go away, or be misled by the treacherous information those people will send on board. Now, if I could steal away without their finding out who I am, they will not suspect that their plans are discovered as they know that the young lord would not understand what had been said." Dermot's great desire therefore was to escape from the cavern. He found that not only was it expected that the country around would rise and attack all the Protestant dwelling-houses in the neighbourhood, but that a French squadron with troops would come off the coast and support their cause.

This, altogether, was terrible news, and Dermot felt that it was most important it should be conveyed without delay to Kilfinnan Castle, the principal seat in that neighbourhood.

Dermot had never liked Father O'Rourke, and he had now still less cause to admire him. He guessed, too, from the character of the man, that although he would encourage the people round to rebel, he was not likely to run himself into danger. He was not surprised, therefore, after hearing him inflame the passions and ardour of his misguided countrymen, to see him quietly take his departure after uttering his blessing and promising them success if they would follow his injunctions.

We must now return to the vicarage. Scarcely had Dermot left the house on the pony, than Miss O'Reilly began to regret that she had allowed him to go. She went to the door and felt the blast blowing keenly from the north, and knowing the lateness of the hour, she feared that he would be benighted long before he could reach the castle.

5

She would willingly have despatched some one to him, but she had no person to send.

While standing at the door, she heard a voice, singing one of the wild and plaintive airs of the country, down in the valley beneath the vicarage. She knew by the sounds that the singer was drawing nearer and nearer the house.

"It is poor mad Kathleen," she said to herself, "though she has but a small amount of brains, yet she is fleet of foot, and would soon overtake the lad, and bring him back to the house. It would be better to do that, than let him go on with the pony he ill knows how to bestride."

The song continued, and in a short time the singer stood in front of the vicarage.

"Well, Kathleen, what brings you here?" asked Miss O'Reilly, addressing her in a kind tone.

"What brings me here takes me wherever I list to go, my own free will," answered the mad girl, who was still young, and possessed of an amount of beauty which made those who saw her feel even more sympathy and compassion than they might have done, had her appearance been less attractive.

"You are good and kind, Kathleen," said Miss O'Reilly; "you would do me a kindness, I know, if I were to ask you."

"That I would, lady!" answered the girl, in the

broken Saxon which was spoken by not many of the peasantry in that part of Ireland; "I would do anything to serve you, just say what it is."

Miss O'Reilly, in a few words, explained to Kathleen what she wished to have done.

"You know him, you know young Dermot O'Neil?"

"O yes, I know him well; he is a gentle lad and a good one, and I would gladly serve him, as I would you, lady."

Miss O'Reilly again endeavoured to impress upon the wandering mind of the poor girl what she was to do, and then begged her to hasten off to overtake Dermot. However, neither she nor Miss O'Reilly were aware of the distance Dermot would have got before Kathleen could overtake him.

The mad girl went singing on as was her wont for some time, till suddenly she became unusually silent.

She had not gone far when she heard the loud talking of a body of men approaching her.

"Those voices at this time of the evening bode no good," she said to herself. "They are some of the rebels who they say are about the country. I never loved such. I will hide and watch to see what they are about."

She accordingly concealed herself among the

rocks and uneven ground with which the road was bounded. The tramp of feet approached, coming from the direction of the castle, and she saw some men leading a pony on which a lad was mounted, hurriedly proceeding towards the north.

From what she had heard from Miss O'Reilly, she at once concluded that the person she had seen in the hands of the insurgents must be Dermot himself.

"Now the next thing I have to do," she thought, "is to follow and try to find out where they are taking him to. Surely they will not do him an injury, but still they have no right to carry him off; of that I am certain."

Gathering her cloak around her, she quickly followed the footsteps of the party she had seen pass.

She had to keep at a cautious distance, lest in crossing any open space, she might have been discovered, but where a person in their right mind might have hesitated, she went on fearlessly. The road was rough and up and down hill, but she continued her pursuit till the party suddenly came to a halt.

"Oh!" she said to herself; "I know the spot where they have gone to; shall I go on, or shall I go back to Miss O'Reilly and tell her how I have been defeated in fulfilling her directions?"

In spite of the distance she determined to follow the latter course.

The astonishment of Miss O'Reilly was very great when, at a late hour in the evening, Kathleen appeared and told her what had befallen young Dermot.

Miss O'Reilly instantly consulted her uncle, who fortunately was at home.

"There is something wrong going forward, at all events," he observed. "But why the rebels should have made Dermot prisoner is more than I can say. However, perhaps you can persuade Kathleen to go back to the cave and endeavour to release him. I don't know what else we can do. In the morning I will ride over to the castle and consult with the Earl. He should be informed that a rising of some sort is on foot through the country, though I do not suppose it is of much consequence."

Kathleen was perfectly ready to undertake the release of Dermot if she could accomplish it, and she promised at all events to enter the cavern and to communicate with him.

"He is a wise lad, and it will be a wise thing to do as he bids me," she observed.

"But you must be weary, Kathleen," said Miss O'Reilly; "you will want some refreshment before you set out again to-night."

"No, no, when the mind's at work the body requires no food," said the mad girl, and she burst forth in a wild song which showed the excitement under which she was labouring.

CHAPTER V.

WITHOUT waiting for further directions, away went the mad girl over moorland and glen at a speed which, considering the darkness, scarcely a wild deer could have rivalled, and before long she stood at the entrance of the cavern. She waited for some time in hopes that the inmates would go to sleep, and that she could more easily find an entrance. Listening, she heard voices within, and that of Father O'Rourke above all the rest.

"Where the priest is, there there's mischief," she said to herself. "If he's going to stay there's little I shall be able to do."

She had not waited long, however, concealed behind a rock, when she saw Father O'Rourke issue forth and take his way down the hill. She waited some time longer, then quietly entered the cavern, gliding past the table and up to its further end. The men, who were still awake, gazed at her with astonishment, wondering what had brought her there, but none ventured to speak to her. She was

held in a sort of superstitious reverence by the
ignorant peasantry; and seeing her fearlessly enter,
they fancied that she had authority for coming
among them. No one suspected, indeed, that she
would not prove faithful to their cause, had she discovered their intention. Silently she passed up the
cavern and sat herself down on a chest at the further end, where, concealed by the darkness, she yet
could look forth on the objects lighted by the lamp,
and make her observations.

She had not been there long before she discovered Dermot resting on his elbow on the bunk
where he had been placed. She watched till those
around her appeared to be asleep, and she then
noiselessly glided up to where he lay.

"I have come to look for you, Dermot," she whispered. "Have you any message to send to friends,
or would you have me set you free? The message
I might take, but if I were to try and set you free, -
I might be made prisoner myself."

"I will send a message; that will be the safest
plan," said Dermot. "But how did you find me
out?" She told him briefly.

"Stay, I can take a leaf from one of my books,"
he observed. "I will write it, it will be safer, and
you will remember to deliver it, Kathleen, if you
wish to do me and others real service."

"Oh yes, Dermot, write, you may trust me; it is better than putting it into my poor mind, though I can remember if it is not overcharged," she answered with a sigh. "But be quick, or some of these people will be suspecting us."

Dermot sat up. He had fortunately a pencil in his pocket, and taking a leaf from one of his books, he wrote a few lines, addressed to the Earl, telling him of the intention of the rebels to attack his castle, and also of their purpose of getting the frigate out of the way.

The note may not have been well written or very well expressed, but it was clear and to the purpose. After signing his name he added, "Oh, trust me, my lord, I would come myself but I am a prisoner, and I pray heaven that this may reach you in time to be of service."

Kathleen placed the note in her bosom, hoping that she had not been observed.

"Now hasten away, Kathleen," whispered Dermot. "You can do as much good as I could have done had I been free, and providing those in the castle are preserved I care not what happens."

Kathleen returned to her former seat and began chanting one of the airs she was generally heard singing, and then, once more gliding down the centre of the cave, she took her departure unquestioned by any of the rebels. Again in the open air she quickly descended the mountain, dark as it was, and in spite of the roughness of the way, she hastened forward at a rapid speed towards Kilfinnan Castle. All was silent as she approached the gates. In vain she walked round and round, she could find no means of making herself heard. The inmates, unsuspicious of danger, were all at rest. She looked down into the bay. The frigate was not there. "All my labours will be of no avail," she thought to herself, "if I cannot let the good lord know what is threatened."

She had walked some way under the castle walls, when, looking up, she saw a light in the window. Instantly she gave forth one of her wild songs. Some of those within who had heard of the famed Banshee were fully persuaded that it was a phantom visitor singing outside the gates, indicative of the speedy death of some one of consequence within. At length the window opened.

"Who's there?" asked a feminine voice. "Surely it is some mortal, and not a spirit from another world."

"I'm sure it is," said another voice.

"It's the poor girl Miss O'Reilly was telling us about. What is it you want, Kathleen?" asked the speaker in a tender tone.

"Is it you who calls me, my lady?" answered Kathleen from below.

"Yes, it is I; what brings you here at this hour of the night?"

"A message—a paper for the Earl, my lady," said the mad girl. "It is from one who would serve him, and it is of great importance he told me. I cannot say more now; but if you will let me into the castle I will place it in your hands, and tell you all I know."

"Come round to the front door," said a voice, which was that of Lady Sophy. "We will come down with a light, and admit you."

Some time was occupied by the young ladies in putting on their dresses, and then arousing the Earl with the information that a message of importance was brought for him, they hastened down stairs.

At first, from the incoherent way in which poor Kathleen spoke, Lady Sophy and Nora could not understand what had occurred. At length the truth dawned upon them, and by the time the Earl appeared, they were able to explain to him what they had learned.

He at once clearly understood that Dermot had been seized by those who intended to carry off his own son; and he felt not a little grateful to the young fisher-boy for the way he had behaved in the matter. He saw likewise that no time was to be lost, and that it would be necessary both to send off messengers to procure troops from the nearest place where they were quartered, and also immediately to put the castle into a state of defence. He regretted the absence of the frigate, and could only hope that she might return sooner than it had been Captain Falkner's intention of doing.

In vain Lady Sophy pressed poor Kathleen, after her exertions, to remain and rest at the castle.

"No, no," she answered; "I will be back again at my home. If I am absent, they will suspect that I have taken a part in this matter; and though they can do me no harm, they may injure those I love."

The poor girl could scarcely be persuaded to take any refreshment; and at length, having eaten a little which Lady Nora brought her, she hastened away towards the vicarage, singing in her usual strain as she went.

The Earl quickly aroused the inmates of the castle. Messengers were sent off as he proposed, and all the people in the neighbourhood who could be trusted were summoned to come within the walls to aid in its defence. There were a few guns planted on the battlements, but they were more for show than use, that part of the country having hitherto been tranquil, and no idea being entertained that they would be required. There were, however, muskets and pistols in the armoury, and pikes, and numerous old weapons of warfare which were stored there, more as an exhibition on account of their antiquity than for use. Still, the gates were strong, and it would require no small amount of force to break them open.

The preparations for the defence occupied a considerable time: the lower windows had to be barricaded, and the doors strengthened by stout bars. A few holes were left for musketry in different parts, and a supply of large stones was brought up from the beach below to serve as missiles, should the rebels approach near enough to make them useful.

The first streaks of daylight were appearing in the sky before all these preparations were made. Soon after, while the little garrison were resting from the toil they had undergone, the tramp of feet was heard approaching the castle.

CHAPTER VI.

TOWARDS morning Dermot was roused from the bunk on which he had been placed by the man who had before spoken, and an intimation given him that he must rise and prepare to move.

He again saw the person who had been called O'Higgins marshalling the rebels, giving various directions, and finally putting himself at their head, as in regular order they marched away from the cavern.

On being led out of the cave Dermot was placed on the pony and led between two men, and was conducted at a rapid pace towards the south. He knew this by finding the wind still in his back, and catching a glimpse through the gloom of the distant sea.

"They must be going back to the castle," he thought, "and are about to make the attack they have been threatening. I hope Kathleen arrived in time; if not, those beautiful young ladies and the kind Earl will fall into their hands. Oh, that I·

could have got away and made sure of giving them warning in time; and yet I do not think the people in the cave slept through the night, and I should have been found out to a certainty. Even now, I don't think they know who I am, and they still believe they have got the young lord. Well, they may hang me in their rage when they find out who I am, and it cannot be helped. Kathleen will scarcely have failed in giving the notice I sent. But then, if they kill me, oh, what grief for my poor mother! That is the bitterest thing in the matter: for her sake, if I thought there was a chance of escaping I would make the attempt; but if God thinks right to call me out of the world, He knows what is best. Still something may occur by which I may hope to escape, though I know these men about me are ready for any bloody work. What fearful oaths I heard them swear, and we know too well what dreadful things have been done in other parts of the country. The young and the fair, and the old and the helpless, have been murdered by their cruel hands. A fearful thing is this civil war. I used not to think much of it once, but I do now. And oh, that sweet young Lady Nora and her cousin, to think of the horrors to which they may be exposed."

Such were the thoughts which passed rapidly

through Dermot's brain in spite of the danger to which he himself was exposed. He heard the people as before speaking round him in the native Irish, but he took good care to make no remarks; indeed, he felt sure that should he speak, his voice alone might betray him. Had they indeed seen him in daylight they might have suspected, in spite of the cloak which covered him, that he was not the young lord. At length he knew by the appearance of the country, and the expressions he heard uttered round him, that they were drawing close to the castle, though they had arrived by a more inland route than that which he usually took. He judged that some hundreds of people comprised the force of rebels. They were armed in a variety of ways, but a considerable number had muskets and pistols. He discovered also that the two small field-pieces which he had seen in the cavern had been brought with them. Not knowing the moderate powers of such pieces of ordnance, he was afraid that the insurgents with them would batter down walls. This made him feel more alarmed than ever for the safety of his friends.

The rebel force now drew up close round the castle, and a consultation was held among the chiefs as to how the attack should be commenced.

Dermot was led up on his pony close to where

the leaders were assembled holding their consultation of war. One of them, with more sagacity than
the rest, suggested that before they began the
attack they should demand the surrender of the
fortress, threatening that if this was not agreed to,
they would immediately put to death the young
lord whom they had in their power.

One of their number was accordingly selected to
act as herald, and directed to proceed to the front
gate, and to demand a parley. The man thus honoured was a broad-shouldered Celt, evidently more
accustomed to dig than to perform the part for
which he had been appointed. He was furnished,
however, with a stick and white handkerchief fas-
tened to it, to act as a flag of truce, and urged to
proceed at once on his mission.

He evidently did not like the task imposed on
him, for Dermot heard him explain that he was
doubtful whether he could muster a sufficient
amount of Saxon to speak to the garrison.

"Never fear that," was the answer; "there are
many who know Celtic inside, and they'll not fail to
understand you."

While these arrangements were being made the
dawn broke. The herald appeared before the gate,
and was considerably astonished when told, in
reply to his demand, that the Earl declined holding

6

any communication with men in arms against their sovereign. "But if we hang the Earl's son if they don't let us in, what will he say to that?" asked the herald.

"You will commit any outrage at your own peril," was the answer. "The Earl knows that you would not dare to hang his son, even if you had him in your power. Do you expect to escape the vengeance of the whole nation should you venture to commit any such atrocity. Go back from whence you came; the Earl and all within this castle set you at defiance."

The herald, unwilling to go back to his companions with such an answer, again asked if such was their ultimate resolution.

"Yes. You will only bring destruction on your own head if you remain where you are; and we again tell you, we defy you," answered the person within.

At last the herald returned to the council of war, which was still sitting. The two guns were now brought forward and placed on an elevated situation, for it had not occurred to their possessors that the only service they could render would be to batter in the gates of the castle. The men who had muskets made their appearance in the front rank, thus to produce a more imposing effect. While these arrangements were being made some of the men had been cutting down young trees in a plantation close by. These they now fixed in a mound near the spot where the guns were posted, and to their tops they secured a cross beam. A rope was then produced.

"We shall have to hang the boy if the Earl does not give in," Dermot heard some of the people round about him observe.

"I would gladly have escaped the work," remarked another. "Yet if it must be done, it must be."

Dermot watched these proceedings, and it would have been unnatural if he had not felt a sensation of horror creeping over him. Should he endeavour to save his life by declaring that he was not the Earl's son. It naturally occurred to him to do this, and yet it would probably no longer avail him. He nerved himself for the fate which seemed inevitable. The preparations had been seen from the castle.

"If you commit murder," shouted a voice from one of the turrets, "you will bring down the vengeance of Heaven and of your country on your heads."

The chiefs continued their consultation. The discussion appeared to be a warm one. Some of them got up and walked about shaking their fists at the castle.

"It must be done!" he heard several exclaim; "it will strike terror into the hearts of our Saxon persecutors. The boy must die. If we let him escape they would declare that we were afraid, and that would make them tyrannize more than ever over us." Several men now came to Dermot and led him towards the gallows which he had seen erected. At the same time an attempt was made to fire the guns placed on the height, but neither of them went off."

"The powder is bad," Dermot thought to himself; "will it all be like that?"

It was a curious thought at such a moment. He had nerved his heart for the worst.

"Again we ask, will you yield the castle?" exclaimed several voices from the height.

"No, but if you injure that boy, vengeance will overtake you," was the answer.

The men uttered a hoarse laugh with some fearful oaths.

"We shall soon see that. Bring him forward. Now, boy, are you prepared for heaven? You will be there in a few minutes. But who are you?" exclaimed several voices.

Before Dermot could reply, the cloak he had

hitherto worn fell from his shoulders, and his dress and appearance showed that he was a very different person to the young lord, whom they fancied they had captured.

None of those present, however, seemed to know him. "If he belongs to these parts he must understand what we have said," exclaimed O'Higgins, "and if so, he may have gained more of our secrets than he should know, a sufficient reason, if there were no other, to hang him. Who are you?" again asked O'Higgins; "say, boy."

"I am the son of Widow O'Neil," he answered, without trepidation, in the native Irish in which he was addressed, "and I am her mainstay and support. If you hang me you will bring the malediction of Heaven, and the widow's curse will rest upon you. If I know your secrets, I am not about to divulge them; I am too much of an Irishman to do that, if I give you my promise that I will not."

This answer seemed to have gained the good opinion of some of the bystanders, but suddenly a man who recognized Dermot sprang up from among them.

"He has become a young heretic; he goes to the house of the Protestant minister, you can never trust him after that," he exclaimed.

"He knows our secrets, and it is dangerous that

he should possess them," observed two or three of the leaders, "and it is evidently necessary to put him out of the way."

Again there was a warm discussion among them, and the remarks of most of the speakers were evidently averse to him.

"He must die—he must die!" exclaimed several voices, and Dermot found himself once more hurried close up to the gallows.

The brutal fellow who had been selected to act as herald, provoked by the reception he had met with, undertook to act as executioner. Dermot's arms were bound tightly behind him, and he was again placed on the pony from which he had dismounted. The rope was secured to the beam, and the savage remorselessly prepared to adjust it round his neck.

WIDOW O'NEIL SAVES HER SON.

CHAPTER VII.

IN another minute the young boy would have
been put out of the world by his savage countrymen, when a loud cry was heard, and a woman
was seen rushing towards the spot. A red cloak
was over her shoulders; her long dark hair streamed
in the wind.

"Who is it you are going to kill? Hold, hold,
you savages!" she exclaimed in native Irish.
"Why, that is my own boy, the son of my bosom.
What harm could one so young and innocent as he
is have done to you? Which of you will dare to
take the widow's only child from her? Which of
you will dare to commit a crime at which the most
cruel of savages would hesitate? Dark curses will
rest upon your bodies here, and on your souls for
ever, if you dare to do so foul a deed. Would any
of you wish to bring down the bereaved widow's
maledictions on your heads? Let the boy go; he
would never wish to harm one of you; a true-hearted
Irish lad." She rushed forward, no one venturing to

stop her. Like a tigress she flew at the man who held the rope in his hand and cast it off the neck of her son. "Now let him go," she exclaimed, throwing out her arm; "I defy you all. Would any one dare to touch him?" With frantic gesture she released his arms which had been bound behind him. "Now let the minister's pony return to its home; he is far too good a beast to serve any one of you. Come with me, Dermot," she exclaimed, as the boy threw himself from the animal and stood by her side. Shielding her son with her cloak, she led him forward, stretching out her arm as if to drive back any who might venture to stop them, and unmolested they took their way towards their home.

The same men who appeared thus abashed and confounded in the presence of a weak woman, now, at the order of O'Higgins, began with all the ferocity of wild beasts, to assault the castle. Again and again they fired their field-pieces with no apparent effect. The men with muskets, however, kept up a hot fire against every part of the building where they thought a bullet might enter. The besieged, however, did not reply to their fire. Not a single person in the castle was to be seen; all apertures were closed, and the shot fell harmlessly against the stone walls.

This determined silence somewhat disconcerted

the rebels, who had expected resistance, and hoped to find some point which they might more easily assail. At length one of their leaders, with more military genius than the rest, proposed bringing the guns down to the front gate. In vain, however, the shots were fired against it; the gates were of iron backed by wood, and the shots made no impression on them. It was then determined to assault the castle by attempting to scale the walls, and the men eagerly set to work to form ladders out of the neighbouring woods. This, however, occupied some time, for although there were plenty of workmen, they had few tools or nails, and after two hours' labour, scarcely two dozen ill-constructed ladders had been formed. With these, however, a band of daring men might possibly gain the battlements.

The object of the assailants was suspected by those within; they prepared accordingly to repel the attack whenever it might be made.

It appeared to the leader of the rebels that by assaulting the south side of the castle they were most likely to prove successful. Thither accordingly he led the main body of his men, while another party continued to assail the front gate, and the remainder, concealed among the walls and rough ground outside the castle, kept up a hot fire on the battlements.   At length the assailants, jumping down into the ditch, placed their ladders against the walls.   Up they began to climb with loud shouts and imprecations on the heads of its defenders.

Unless this last attack should be met by a very determined resistance, there appeared every probability of their succeeding, for could they once gain a lodgment on the walls, they might easily drive the small number of opponents who were likely to be within before them.   A determined band at last led the way, and reached the summit of the walls.   They were there met, however, by a party of the defenders of the castle, led by the Earl himself.   Unaccustomed to the use of swords, the assailants were ill-able to defend themselves, as they attempted to step upon the parapet, while the fire which their friends kept up from the opposite side of the bank, killed several of them, though the bullets failed to strike the defenders; they were therefore quickly hurled down again, and the leading men, falling, struck the others who were attempting to ascend, when all were precipitated into the ditch together, the ladders being dislodged, and thrown down upon the wounded and struggling mass.   They had, however, too nearly succeeded to abandon their project.   They retreated with their ladders, which were soon repaired, when with others in the meantime constructed, a still larger force attempted to scale the walls.

Had we followed the widow and her son, Dermot would have been heard expressing his satisfaction at seeing the white sails of the frigate, which had so lately quitted the harbour, once more approaching the shore, aided by a strong breeze from the north, which still continued to blow. The insurgents were fortunately too much occupied in their attack on the castle to notice her; she was, however, seen by its defenders, and this greatly encouraged them in their resistance. Again the rebels began to climb up their ladders,—this time fully believing they were sure of success. Already a large number were near the summit threatening vengeance on the heads of all who opposed them, when there suddenly arose a cry in their rear, of "the red coats! the red coats." "Ay, and the blue jackets too!" shouted out a loud voice.

"On lads, and drive the rascals into the sea." At this moment a strong party of blue jackets, headed by Captain Falkner, was seen darting forward, while a body of marines followed with fixed bayonets ready to charge. The rebels did not stop to encounter them. Those who were on the ladders leaped hastily down, crushing many below them, and then attempted to seek safety in flight. The marines and blue jackets advanced in double-quick time, clearing all before them. Very few of the rebels offered resistance, and those who did were immediately cut down. Many were taken prisoners, O'Higgins among them, and the rest throwing down their arms, headed by the rest of their chiefs, fled as fast as their legs could carry them into the country. They were pursued for some distance, when, unwilling, to destroy more of the misguided men, Captain Falkner ordered the pursuit to cease, and returned with his followers to the castle. He was received with warm thanks by the Earl. It was extraordinary that not a single person had been hurt within the walls of the castle, though the Earl acknowledged had the rebels once succeeded in gaining the battlements, he could scarcely, with his small garrison, have hoped to defend it against the numbers which would have assailed them. Captain Falkner told him that after he had left the bay, a fishing-boat came alongside with only one man in her, who gave him the information of the proposed rising. Although he did not believe that the castle would be attacked, he had in consequence been induced to return as quickly as possible to an anchorage in the bay, and he was thankful that he had not come back too late.

Part of the marines remained on shore to strengthen the garrison of the castle, and strong parties were sent out in all directions, to ascertain what had become of the rest of the rebels.

A considerable number of the misguided men were captured, but most of their leaders, as is often the case under similar circumstances, managed to effect their escape. The state of the country made it dangerous to send the prisoners overland to Cork, they were, therefore, placed on board the *Cynthia*, to be conveyed there by sea. O'Higgins had contrived to divest himself of part of his dress before he was captured, and owing to this circumstance, he escaped being recognized as one of the leaders of the rebels. Had Dermot been called upon to do so, he would, of course, have been able to identify him; but fortunately for him, no one thought of summoning the fish-wife's young son to give evidence, and he was, therefore, allowed to remain quietly at home.

O'Higgins took the name of Higson, and asserted that he was a pedler travelling through the country, producing a license in confirmation of his statement, but had been compelled by the rebels to join them. Several of the other prisoners were found ready to swear to the truth of this statement. He, however, was found guilty; but instead of being condemned to transportation to Botany Bay, was allowed the privilege of entering as a seaman on board a man-of-war. He accepted the alternative, hoping before long to make his escape. He, however, was too narrowly watched to succeed in his object; and after being sent on board a receiving ship, was curiously enough transferred to the *Cynthia*, on board which frigate we shall soon again hear of him.

From the information Captain Falkner received he had reason to believe that this first attempt of the insurgents having so completely failed, and so many having been made prisoners, or killed, a further rising in that part of the country would not be attempted. Still the disturbed state of the district prevented the ladies from riding about the country as had been their custom, and the Earl would not allow his young son to go to any distance from the walls, nor even a short way without a strong escort.

Young Fitz Barry consoled himself, therefore, by frequent visits on board the frigate, where he soon became a great favourite with the officers. "Ah!" he exclaimed, "I wish my father would let me become a midshipman. I would rather go to sea, than follow any other profession in the world." Those were, perhaps, the most palmy days of England's navy. It was the time when her greatest heroes were flourishing, and the profession was looked upon as among the noblest a youth could follow.

The oftener Fitz Barry visited the frigate, the more anxious he became to belong to her. The midshipmen, at first, encouraged him rather as a joke than in earnest; but as they loved the profession themselves, they were somewhat flattered by finding that the Earl's son wished to join it also. On going on shore one day, he told his father that he had made up his mind to become a sailor. The Earl at first laughed at him, but he had never been in the habit of thwarting his son, and when Fitz Barry assured him that he should pine and perhaps die, unless he was allowed to have his will, the Earl declared that he was a very obstinate boy, but would not throw any objection in his way. Still, as he was not certain that his father was in earnest, he went to Nora and Sophy, to get them to assist in pleading his cause. Lady Sophy having herself made up her mind to marry a sailor, thought that there was not a finer profession to be followed, and Nora, who loved Fitz Barry with all her heart, could not think of doing otherwise than as he wished. Besides, she confessed that a ship was a very beautiful thing, and that she thought her dear brother must be happy on board, for little did the young ladies· know of the toils and dangers, the hardships and the sufferings to which sailors are exposed, whatever their rank. They had read to be sure of wrecks, of noble ships sinking or being burned, of men being castaway on desert islands, with little or no food on which to subsist, of boats long floating on the ocean, till one by one those on board had died of starvation or thirst, or from the exposure they were doomed to endure. To them all was bright and attractive, and Fitz Barry, therefore, by dint of importunity, at length prevailed upon his easy-going father, to allow him to join Captain Falkner's beautiful frigate, the *Cynthia*, provided that officer would take him. That matter he had left in the hands of his cousin, Sophy, and he had no doubt that she would induce the captain to receive him on board. He was perfectly right in his conjectures, for the captain, as many other captains would have been, was very ready to receive an Earl's son among his midshipmen. It was necessary for the frigate to remain for some weeks after the late rising, to ascertain that all was quiet before she could venture to quit the bay.

There was time, therefore, for Barry to be fitted out for sea, and at length, just before the frigate sailed, he·was received on board and rated as a midshipman. He was good-natured and unaffected, was intelligent and zealous in his new profession, had, moreover, plenty of money, and these qualities soon made him a favourite with most of the officers on board.

Captain Falkner having landed his prisoners at Cork, and remained there till their trial was concluded, proceeded on to Plymouth, where the young midshipman was to be provided with the remainder of his outfit. The *Cynthia* was employed for some months as one of the Channel fleet, and during that time had to pay several visits to the coast of Ireland. Captain Falkner did not fail to look into Kilfinnan Bay, and accompanied by Fitz Barry, to pay a visit to the castle. Great was his satisfaction at finding that the family were still there, as he had thus the opportunity of enjoying the society of Lady Sophy. Alas, they little thought how long would be the separation they must after this endure. Barry happened to inquire of his sister what had become of the young fisher-boy who was so nearly hung instead of himself, and he was told that he had disappeared from the place, and that no one knew what had become of him. Such indeed was the case. Not long after the attack of the rebels on the castle, one evening when the widow expected

Dermot to return, he did not make his appearance. In vain she waited the live-long night; no Dermot came back to her. She watched and watched, now she went to the cottage door and stopped to listen; now she hastened down to the boat, that, however, was still moored in its accustomed place. She took her way up to the downs. In vain she called on Dermot; no answer came to her calls. She returned home to mourn and to wonder what had become of her boy. He would not have left his mother without telling her. He loved her too well, she was sure of that, and yet who could have carried him away? Had the rebels done so? That seemed but too likely, for they were too often wont to wreak their vengeance on the heads even of those who could do them no further harm. The morning came and found her still sitting at the open door, waiting for the return of her boy. The sun rose over the rugged hill and shed his rays down into the glen, tinging the points of the rocks on either side, and casting a bright glow over the ocean; still Dermot did not appear. She determined to go forth and search for him, but whither should she go? He might have gone to the castle, but they surely would not have detained him beyond the night, and he must soon then come back. She waited all day, but when the night came on he had not appeared. Weary and sad she sat down on the bench by the fireside, and there at length fell asleep. She awoke by being conscious that some one was present, and looking up saw by the light of the log which still blazed on the hearth, the figure of poor mad Kathleen sitting before her.

"You are sad, widow—you are sad," exclaimed the mad girl; "it is waiting for your son you are; and do you think that he will ever return? It may be he will, but you will have many weary years to wait until then."

"What do you know of my boy?" exclaimed the widow. "Tell me, Kathleen, tell me, girl, has any harm happened to him?"

"No; the harm is that he was weary of home, and has gone far away, so I understand, if my poor brain has not misled me. Here, see, he gave me this, and told me to bring it to you. It will tell you far more than I can; it speaks words, though I cannot understand them."

"No more can I," cried the widow in a tone of grief. "Oh, that he should have gone away and left his poor mother; but maybe in these lines he will have told me why he has gone and when he will come back. Still I do not know that I could have borne the parting from him even had he gone with my consent. But those lines, girl, let me have them; there are others can read them though I cannot. I wish it were the day, that I might go forth and find some one to help me."

The widow took the paper which the mad girl gave her; it was a letter of considerable length. As Dermot knew that his mother could not have read it herself, he must have trusted to her finding some person to perform that office for her.

The widow begged Kathleen to rest in her hut that night, hoping that she might, during the time, gather some more information from her about her son. All she could learn, however, was, that she had met Dermot on the way to the south, some distance beyond the castle, and that he had given her that letter, which he intended otherwise to have sent by the post. Poor Kathleen then launched out in his praises, and declared that she had never seen a lord his equal in these parts. The widow's first impulse was to go and seek for Father O'Rourke, the person to whom the peasantry, whenever they had any document to be read, generally resorted. She remembered, however, his dislike to Dermot and the words of anger with which they had parted from each other, and she therefore felt a repugnance to let him see what her Dermot might have said to her. "Then there is the blind lady," she thought to herself; "she cannot see to read, however.

Then there is the sweet young lady who came here from the castle one day, and the little girl, the Earl's daughter, but they are too grand to care for what a poor boy like Dermot has to say. I will go, therefore, to Mr. Jamieson, and get him to read the letter. He is kind and gentle too, and maybe he will give me a word of comfort about my boy. Still I cannot understand why Dermot should have gone away without saying a word of farewell to his poor old mother."

Kathleen, for a wonder, gladly consented to rest at the widow's cottage till the next morning. They then together took their way to the vicarage. The widow found Mr. Jamieson about to leave the house, yet he kindly stopped to hear what she had to say to him. She presented the letter, and telling him that she had only received it on the previous evening, begged him to read it to her. He at once recognized the handwriting of his pupil.

"Ah, Widow O'Neil," he exclaimed, "I find by this that your son is away, and you must be prepared not to see him for some time. I scarcely like to say that the lad has acted wrongly in what he has done. He tells you, Mrs. O'Neil, how he loves you, that he would die for you, and that his great object is to go into the world, and to make a fortune, and come home and support you. He says that he could not bring himself to go through the pain of wishing you farewell. He would rather go away without saying a word about it, or letting you know what were his intentions, for he is sure you would not have prevented him, and he would do anything to save you and himself from the agony of the parting moment. I believe him, widow. I am sure that he has a gentle and a loving heart, and that he speaks the truth when he gives that as his reason for going away without seeing you. Yet it was to save you, rather than himself, for he must have known when he left his home, that he was gazing his last at you for many a day. Of one thing I am certain, that his heart will not change, his love will not alter, and that wherever he goes, you will be the chief person he will always think of, and that he will look forward to seeing you again, as the greatest joy which can be allowed him on earth." The good minister believed that he spoke the truth, when he thus attempted to comfort the bereaved mother. The widow returned home feeling more consoled than could have been expected, for the loss of Dermot. Kind Miss O'Reilly continued to pay her frequent visits, and while the young ladies remained at the castle, they rode over under an escort several times to see her. They heard with surprise of Dermot's departure, and at first were inclined to think him hard-hearted and ungrateful, but so ably did the widow defend her son, that they soon agreed with her it was but natural a boy like Dermot should seek to see more of the world than he could in that remote part of Ireland.

The *Cynthia* had been stationed for some months on the Irish coast, when she stood for the last time into the bay, before taking her departure.

As Captain Falkner had had an opportunity of letting the Earl know his purpose, a large party were collected at the castle, to bid him and the young hero farewell. Those were the days of profuse Irish hospitality; the gentlemen with their wives and families for many miles around had assembled.

The morning was spent in all sorts of sports, and the evening in conviviality. Frequently a stag was turned out from a neighbouring thicket, when a long run, sometimes across rivers, up and down hills, by the borders of lakes, and over the roughest imaginable ground, took place. Many falls were the consequence, in spite of the sturdy character of the horses, and the admirable riding of the men, but few were present who had not seen a companion dislocate his shoulder, and not unfrequently terminate his career with a broken neck. It was not unusual to see a hundred horses stabled in the castle at a time, some of them belonging to the Earl, but a considerable number to his guests, and the profuse hospitality of those days demanded that all the attendants should be well cared for within the walls of the castle. The dinner hour was somewhat early, that a longer period might be devoted to the after carousal. The cellars usually contained numerous hogsheads of claret, whilst stronger wines and whisky were on hand for those of less refined tastes. But the Irish gentleman rather prided himself on the quantity of claret he could imbibe, and yet be able to retire with steady steps to bed, or if necessary to mount his horse and return home by cross roads without breaking his neck, or finding himself at sunrise just waking out of sleep in a dry ditch.

Although the Earl himself did not over-indulge in the pleasures of the table, he had been too long habituated to the custom to discourage it in others, and thus his legitimate income was inadequate to supply the expenses of the profuse hospitality he kept up.

The ladies retired early from the table, when the slight restraint their presence imposed being removed, the bottle began to circulate even more freely than before. Songs were sung, toasts were given, and the health of the young heir of Kilfinnan was drunk with uproarious cheers. "May he be as fine a man as his father, and an honour to the noble profession he has chosen, though faith! I'd rather he followed it than I myself," exclaimed a red-nosed squire from the lower end of the table. "May he live to see his grandchildren around him, and may the old castle stand as long as the round world endures."

"Sure a finer young sailor never placed foot on the deck of a man-of-war," echoed another landowner of the same stamp. "May he come back a captain at the least, and take the lead in the field in many a hard day's run." Similar compliments were uttered in succession for some time. Fitz Barry took them very quietly, indeed he at length became utterly weary of the proceedings. In truth also, the thoughts of leaving home and his sweet young sister and his cousin Sophy, whom he loved like one, made him somewhat sad, and little able to enter into the conversation going forward. He did not, however, allow either Sophy or Nora to discover how much he felt.

The next morning, farewells over, he went on board the frigate, without much prospect of returning home for three years or more. As she under all sail stood out of the bay, he cast many a lingering glance at the old castle, and the well-known bold outlines of the shore. At Plymouth, to which port the frigate had been ordered to proceed, several fresh hands were entered to make up the complement of her proper crew. They were of all descriptions, but Captain Falkner soon discovered that there was scarcely a seaman among them. Officers in those days, when men were scarce, had to form their crews out of the most heterogeneous materials. He was receiving a report of them from his first lieutenant. "Here is a fellow, sir. He has been sent to us from the tender, and has entered under the name Higson, and says he is an Englishman, though he is evidently Irish by his tongue, and the cut of his features and general appearance from head to foot. He knows little enough of a seaman's duties, but is a stout, strong fellow, and we may in time lick him into shape. I am advised to keep an eye on him while we remain in harbour, lest he should take French leave, and forget to return on board."

"We must keep him," answered the captain; "we are bound for the West Indies, you know, and shall require every man we can lay hold of."

This settled the point—O'Higgins the rebel leader, or rather Higson, as he called himself, was regularly entered on the books of the *Cynthia*. He, in vain, made several efforts to escape; once he narrowly escaped being shot in the attempt. He had jumped into a boat at night, and was pulling away from the ship when he was overtaken, and being brought back was put into irons till the frigate sailed. Had he been in Cork harbour, he would have had little difficulty in effecting his purpose. Hearing, however, that a son of the Earl of Kilfinnan was on board, he consoled himself with the reflection that he should have an opportunity of wreaking his vengeance on the head of the midshipman. How the lad had in any way given him cause of offence, none but a distorted imagination could have supposed. He had certainly attempted for a very indefinite object of his own to burn down the Earl's residence and to murder the inhabitants, and because he had been foiled in the attempt, captured and punished, he persuaded himself that he was fully justified, in desiring to kill or injure the Earl's unoffending son. Such, however, was the style of reasoning in which so-called Irish patriots of those days, and, perhaps, in later times, were apt to indulge.

At length, powder and stores having been received on board, and two or three gun-room officers and several passed midshipmen having joined, the *Cynthia* made sail, and standing out of the harbour, a course was shaped for the West Indies, her destined station.

The frigate had been for some time at sea, and during a light wind she fell in with a homeward bound merchantman. These were the days of the press-gang, and under such circumstances every merchantman was visited, that the seamen on board who had not a protection might be carried off to serve in the Royal Navy. This was a cruel regulation, but, at the same time, it seemed the only feasible one to our forefathers for manning the king's ships. Often good men were thus picked up, but more frequently bad and discontented ones. The merchant ship was ordered to heave to, and the second lieutenant, with a boat's crew armed to the teeth, went on board. The whole of the crew were directed to come up on deck. Their names were called over, and three able seamen were found who did not possess a protection. They were immediately ordered to go over the side into the boat.

"Are there any others who wish to volunteer on board?" asked the lieutenant. There was some hesitation among them, when two youngsters stepped forward in front of the rest. The master endeavoured to prevent them from speaking; but the lieutenant telling them to say what they wished, they at once begged that they might be allowed to join the frigate. They were both fine active-looking lads, and seemed cut out to make first-rate seamen. The lieutenant eyed them with approbation.

"You will do, my lads," he observed. "In a couple of years or less, you will make active topmen."

The master was very indignant at being thus deprived of part of his crew; but he had no remedy, and was obliged to submit.

" A pleasant voyage to you, Captain Dobson," said the lieutenant. "You will manage to find your way up Channel without these few men I have taken from you, and depend upon it they will be better off than they would have been spending their time at Wapping until all their money was gone;" a truth which even the master could not deny.

The merchantman sailed on her way, and the boat having returned on board the frigate, was hoisted up again, when her sails being trimmed, the *Cynthia* once more stood on her course. The new-comers soon made themselves at home with the crew. Those who watched the lads might have seen an expression of astonishment pass over the countenance of one of them when he found himself on board the *Cynthia*. Soon after this they were brought up before the first lieutenant, to undergo the usual examination. He soon finished with the men, who had the ordinary account to give of themselves. One of the young lads said he belonged to Dartmouth in England, and that having run away from home he had joined the merchantman, from which he had volunteered, and he was entered by the name of Ned Davis.

"And what is your name, my lad?" he asked, turning to the youngest of the two.

"Charles Denham, sir," he answered.

"That is an English name, and you speak with an Irish accent."

"My mother was an Irish woman," answered the lad, with a blush on his face.

"And who was your father, then?" asked the lieutenant.

"Sir, I came on board to serve his Majesty, and I hope to do so faithfully," replied the lad, as if he had not heard the question put to him.

"There is some of the true metal in that boy," observed the first lieutenant, turning to an officer near him. "I must keep an eye upon him. He will make a smart seaman in a short time. He is just one after the captain's own heart."

The young volunteer did not hear these observations, or they would have given him the encouragement of which he somewhat felt the want. The lads were told their numbers and the mess to which they would belong. Ned Davis and Charles Denham returned together to the lower deck. They found, after they had been some time below, that the crew were far from satisfied with their officers. They discovered that the ringleader was a certain John Higson, who was ready to find fault with everything that took place. He was what is generally called at sea, "a king's hard bargain," or in other words, not worth his salt. He was one of those men who do a great deal of mischief on board a ship, and are generally known by the name of "a sea lawyer." The two lads, however, seemed resolved to do their duty in spite of anything that might occur. They had before, it appeared, heard Captain Falkner spoken of, and knew he had the character of being a just officer, though somewhat strict. It soon appeared, indeed, that he had a very unruly ship's company to deal with, and one that required a good deal of management to bring into order. Had it not been for Higson, and other men like him, this might easily have been accomplished; but whatever was done Higson was sure to put a wrong interpretation upon it. Still the best men found themselves well treated, and spoken kindly to by their officers. By degrees flogging decreased, though occasionally some were brought up to suffer that punishment. In those days an officer might order it to be inflicted on any one of the crew, and sometimes this was done for slight offences. Captain Falkner, however, reserved it for those who seemed determined to neglect their duty, or to get drunk, or to act disrespectfully to their officers. Higson was himself too clever ever to get punished, though more than once he was the cause of others becoming sufferers. At length the West Indies were reached, and the frigate brought up in Kingston Harbour, Jamaica.

Unfortunately, Captain Falkner was taken ill, and it became necessary for him to go and reside on shore. The first lieutenant, though a kind officer, had not the talent of his superior, and thus the ship once more fell into the condition in which it had previously been. It being found that Captain Falkner did not recover, the admiral of the station ordered the *Cynthia* to put to sea under the command of the first lieutenant. She cruised for some time in search of an enemy, but none was to be found, and sickness breaking out on board, a good many of the men were laid up in their hammocks. Meantime, young Lord Fitz Barry had become a great favourite with his brother officers on board. Indeed, from his youth he was somewhat of a pet among them. He was not a little made of by the first lieutenant and the other officers, not so much because he was a lord, but because he was a kind-hearted, generous little fellow. He had, however, been imbued by his captain with very strict notions of duty, and, young as he was, when sent away with a boat's crew he kept them in as strict order as any of the older midshipmen could have done. On one occasion when sent on shore to bring off wood and water from an uninhabited part of the southern shore of St. Domingo, some of his boat's crew insisted on going up into the interior. His orders had been not to allow them to go out of sight of the boat, and should any person appear from the shore, immediately to shove off and return to the ship. When, however, they were told by Fitz Barry to remain where they were, they laughed at him, and began to move off into the country. He instantly drew a pistol from his belt, and hastened after them, threatening to shoot the nearest man if they did not instantly return. Still they persevered, and according to his threat the young lord fired his pistol, and hit one of the mutineers in the arm, and immediately drawing a second pistol he threatened to treat another in the same way. This brought the mutineers to reason, and turning round they sulkily followed him towards the boat. Here the wounded man insisted on having his revenge, and tried to persuade the rest of the boat's crew to throw the young lord overboard.   The two lads who had come on board from the merchantman had been appointed to the boat, both of them by this time being strong enough to pull an oar.   They, however, instead of siding with the rest of the crew, had remained in the boat, and declared that if a hand was laid upon Lord Fitz Barry, they would denounce the rest to their commander.

"And we will heave you youngsters overboard with him," exclaimed the men, enraged at being thus opposed.

"At your peril," answered Charles Denham; "I am not one to be cowed by your threats.   The man who was shot only got his deserts, and it will serve you all right if Lord Fitz Barry reports you when he gets on board."

This plain speaking still further enraged the rest of the boat's crew.   At the same time, unless they had been prepared to kill their young officer and the two lads, they had no resource but to submit. They had pulled off some little distance from the shore when they again threatened to throw all three overboard, unless they would promise not to report them.   This Lord Fitz Barry refused to do.

"No," he said, keeping the other pistol in his hand.   "It is for me to command you.   You dis-obeyed orders and now must take the consequences."

He reflected that if he returned and let their conduct go unpunished, it might lead to still more serious disobedience. He, therefore, as soon as he got on board, reported the whole affair to the commanding officer, at the same time taking care to praise the two lads who had so bravely stood by him. The consequence was, that the whole of the boat's crew were brought to the gangway and severely flogged.

CHAPTER VIII.

THE effect of the severe, though just, punishment inflicted on the boat's crew who had misbehaved themselves under the command of Lord Fitz Barry was to produce much ill-will among a considerable number of the crew, increased, as before, by Higson's instigations. The officers were not aware, however, of what was taking place. The men, although sometimes exhibiting sulky looks when ordered about their duty, continued to perform it as usual. The two young volunteers, it appeared, had been better brought up than the generality of seamen. Both, from their earliest days, had been accustomed to offer up a prayer before turning in at night. This practice on board a man-of-war it was very difficult, if not almost impossible, to keep up. They agreed, however, that they would steal down when they could to the fore-part of the orlop deck, and there, in a quiet corner near the boatswain's store-room, they might have the opportunity of kneeling down together, and offering up their prayers in silence. This practice they had continued unsuspected for some time. In those days such a thing was almost unheard of on board a man-of-war. At the present time, however, there are not only many praying seamen on board ship, but prayer meetings are often held, and a very considerable number of some ships' crews are now able to join them.

On one occasion, after it had been blowing hard, and the lads had been aloft for a considerable time, they were both very weary, and after kneeling down and offering up their prayers as usual, they leaned back, sitting on the coils of a cable, with the intention of talking together. In a short time, however, both fell asleep. How long they slept they did not know, but they were awoke by hearing voices near them; without difficulty they recognized the speakers. Higson was among the principal of them; they listened attentively; had they been discovered, they felt sure, from what they heard, that their lives would have paid the forfeit. It was proposed to seize the ship and put the officers on shore, or should they offer any resistance to kill them, as had in another instance been done, and then after going on a buccaneering cruise, to carry the ship into an American port and sell her, the men hoping to get on shore to enjoy their ill-gotten booty.

A few years before this a large portion of the English fleet had mutinied, but they had had many causes of complaint; still their crime was inexcusable. Most of the ringleaders suffered punishment, and the crews were pardoned. This lesson seemed to be lost, however, upon Higson and his associates. They had inflamed each other's minds with descriptions of the pleasures they would enjoy on shore, and of the hardships they had at present to undergo. The young lads dared not move. Every moment they expected to be discovered. Some of the mutineers, more sanguine than the rest, expressed their determination to wreak their vengeance upon those who had chiefly offended them, and young Lord Fitz Barry, with several others, were singled out to undergo the punishment of death. The first lieutenant also was to be among their victims. The lads could not tell what hour it was, nor how long they would have to remain in their present position. They dreaded that the mutineers would instantly go on deck and carry out their nefarious plans. Young Denham's chief wish was to hurry off and warn those who had been chiefly threatened. "If the officers have time to show a bold front, the men will not dare to act against them," he thought; "but if they are taken by surprise, the mutineers will treat them as wild beasts treat the animals which they have caught in their clutches, and will be sure to tear them in pieces. If they once get the upper hand, they will kill them all, just as they did in the ship I have heard of, when scarcely one officer was allowed to escape." At length they heard the morning watch called, and not till then did the mutineers leave the place. The lads waited till they believed that everybody was on deck, and then cautiously climbing up the ladder, stole away to their own hammocks. As the middle watch was only then turning in, they were not observed, and they lay there till they concluded that all those surrounding them had gone to sleep. Denham then proposed going and warning the officers. Ned Davis begged that he himself might go.

"No," said Denham, "I will go alone and tell the commander what I have heard." Denham had scarcely got as far as the door of the captain's cabin, now occupied by the first lieutenant, when the sentry stopped him.

"You cannot pass here," he said putting him back as he, in his eagerness, pressed on.

"But I tell you I have a matter of importance to speak to the commander about," said Denham boldly. "It will be at your own risk if you stop me."

"You can tell one of the other officers in the gun-room," said the sentry.

"No; it is for the commanding officer alone," responded Denham. "I will speak to him only."

Just then the first lieutenant himself appeared at the door.

"I want to speak to you, sir," said Denham eagerly.

"Come in. What is it about?" inquired the first lieutenant.

"If you will go where no one else will hear me, I will tell you, sir."

The lieutenant retired into the inner cabin.

"Now, what is it, my lad?" he asked.

Denham then told him of the plot to which he had become privy, for taking the ship from the officers. In later days such information would have been laughed at, but unhappily in those days such occurrences had become too frequent to allow the commanding officer to disbelieve his statements.

"Stay here, my lad," said the first lieutenant, "if you go forward again, and the men suspect you of having informed against them, you will be among the first victims."

Arming himself with a brace of pistols, and taking his sword in his hand, he went into the gun-room. He here aroused the officers and telling them what he had heard, ordered them immediately to repair on deck, sending some of them to call up the midshipmen and the warrant officers. The marines were then ordered to muster on deck under arms, while several of the petty officers whom it was known could be trusted were also called aft; a guard was then placed over the magazine, and the two after guns were hauled in and trained forward. These preparations were made so suddenly and quietly that even the watch on deck were scarcely aware of what was going forward. There was no time to lose, for while those preparations were going on, Ned Davis, who had been on the watch, made his way aft with the information that a number of the men were collecting together forward, armed with all the weapons they could lay hold of, and that from the threats they were uttering they evidently intended to make a sudden dash aft, in the expectation of surprising the officers before they had left their berths. It was very evident that they would have done so had it not been for the warning conveyed by Denham.

When the sun, as it does in those latitudes, suddenly burst above the waters, and darkness rapidly gave place to daylight, the officers and the marines were found drawn up on the quarter deck, and the mutineers who, at that moment, made a sudden rush aft along the main deck, found themselves confronted by a body of marines, who issued from the gun-room; others who came along the upper deck also saw that their plot was discovered, and that they had not a hope of success. The drum then beat to quarters, and all hands were summoned on deck. The first lieutenant now stepping forward, exclaimed, "What is it you want, my lads? if you are treated with injustice, say so. If you have anything else to complain of, let me know, but, as you see, your mutinous intentions are discovered, and let me tell you that those who are guilty will receive the punishment which they merit." Not a man spoke in return for some time. At length several coming aft, declared they knew nothing about the intentions of the rest, when it was found that the mutineers consisted chiefly of the Irish rebels who had been put on board at Cork, and of a few smugglers and jail-birds who had been won over by Higson.

"Some of you will grace the yard-arm before long," observed the first lieutenant, "but I intend to give you another trial. I have no wish that any man should die for this day's work, however richly some of you may deserve it. Those who prove faithful to their duty will find that they are rewarded, and those who act as traitors to their king and country will discover, too late, that they will not go unpunished. Now pipe below."

The mutiny which at first threatened such serious consequences, by the determination of the first lieutenant was then happily quelled, and the ship soon after returned to Port Royal. Here Captain Falkner was found sufficiently recovered to resume his command. The men soon discovered that he had been informed of the mutiny. He told the men so in very explicit terms. Adding—

"You have brought disgrace on yourselves, men, and on the ship in a way which makes me ashamed of you, but I hope before long, that we shall fall in with an enemy, and that then I shall find you wipe it out, by the gallantry of your conduct." The men on hearing these words, cheered their captain, and from that day forth he had no cause to complain of the general conduct of the ship's company. They were continually on the look-out for an enemy's cruiser. Several merchant vessels were taken and sent into port, and a small brig-of-war was captured, without having fired a shot in her own defence. The midshipmen were always encouraged by their captain to exercise themselves by running aloft over the mast-head, and sliding down by the different ropes which led on deck. Sometimes the game of follow my leader was played; the most active lad leading the way. Now to the mizen-mast-head, next to the main-top-gallant-mast-head, and so on to the fore-mast, and finally, perhaps down to the bow-sprit end. Now like monkeys, they were seen to run out on the yard-arms, and it seemed wonderful that they could, at the rate they went, escape falling. On one occasion, during a game, both the midshipmen and the ship's boys were thus amusing themselves. Several of the top-men were on the main-top-mast yard. A sudden splash was heard. "A man overboard!" was the cry. Quick as lightning a ship's boy was seen gliding down a backstay. As he touched the hammock-nettings, instead of jumping down on deck, he plunged overboard.

"A shark! a shark!" was heard, uttered in tones of horror by several voices on deck. The order was given to lower a boat. Gratings and oars and spars were hove overboard. A short way from the ship, a young fair face was seen floating upwards, while Charles Denham, who it appeared had sprung overboard, was striking out rapidly towards him. The attention of all on board was directed to the spot. Had it not been for fear of the voracious monster of the deep, many might have jumped overboard to assist, still they shouted and kept throwing in things, to distract, if possible, the attention of the shark from the lad in the water. Denham knowing well the enemy he had to contend with, continued striking the water with all his might with his feet, as he swam forward, shouting at the same time. But young Lord·Fitz Barry, for it was he who had tumbled overboard, lay perfectly unconscious, and it seemed too probable would become a prey to the monster. Already its dark fin was seen not far off, but the boat had now touched the water, and an eager crew was pulling towards the lads. Denham's hand was already under the head of the young lord, whom he supported while he struck out with his feet and other hand. A shark, however ferocious, will seldom attack a person who is in constant movement, and by his shouts and splashing, Denham thus contrived to keep the monster at a distance. The boat approached. Those in the bows leant over to drag in the young lord.

"Never mind me," exclaimed Denham, as he helped to lift him into the boat.

"But we must mind you," answered a man, "or that brute will have you even now."

Denham's hands were on the gunnel of the boat, when the black fin, at a short distance off disappeared under the water. A strong, tall topman was standing in the boat. He leaned over, and seizing Denham in his arms lifted him up; but scarcely had his feet got above the surface, when the monster's enormous pair of jaws were seen to rise close to it. Young Denham was saved, but few have run a greater risk of losing their lives. In the meantime the young lord lay unconscious in the bow of the boat.

"We must get him on board at once," exclaimed the officer who had come in her. "He is alive though, and must be put under the doctor's care."

The boat immediately returned on board. It was found that Lord Fitz Barry had fallen upon his side when dropping into the water, and that the whole of that part of his body was for the time paralyzed. Still, in a short time he returned to consciousness, but some time elapsed before he had recovered. His chief anxiety seemed to be to express his gratitude to the lad who had saved him. Denham modestly replied that he had only done his duty, though he was not insensible of the young lord's kind feelings.

When Lord Fitz Barry was sufficiently recovered the captain invited him, as was the custom, to dine at his table, and the subject of his fall was alluded to.

"If you can do me a favour, sir," he observed, "and in any way reward the boy who saved my life, I should indeed be grateful. There is something in him which prevents me from venturing to offer him money. I am sure he would prize promotion of some sort more than anything else. He seems to me as he walks the deck to be superior to all the other lads, and to be more like a gentleman than any of them."

"We will keep an eye on him, Fitz Barry," answered the captain, with a smile. "I have watched him on many occasions; and if I understand rightly, this is not the first time he has rendered you a service. What do you say? Shall we place him on the quarter-deck? What would your mess-mates say to that?"

"There is not one of them who would not be pleased, sir," answered the young lord. "They all think well of him; and since that boat affair, when, I believe, if it had not been for him, those villians would have hurled me overboard, they have all wished that he would get some reward."

"He was the lad, sir, who gave me the information of the intended mutiny, so that really, I believe, he was the means of preserving all our lives, and preventing fearful disgrace being brought upon the service," observed the first lieutenant.

"Well, I do not like to make such promotions in a hurry," answered the captain; "but from what I have heard of the lad, if he is found to possess a fair amount of education, I shall be very glad to offer him the opportunity of being placed on the quarter-deck."

"But he looks to me such a clever fellow," said Lord Fitz Barry, "that I am sure he will soon learn to read and write, if he cannot now."

The captain talked the matter over for some time with the first lieutenant, and it was arranged that the young volunteer should forthwith be placed in the midshipman's berth. To Fitz Barry's infinite satisfaction, next morning, after divisions, while all the officers were assembled on the quarter-deck, Charles Denham was summoned aft.

"Charles Denham is, I believe, your name," said the captain. "You have on more than one occasion done good service since you joined this ship, besides which, your general conduct is unexceptionable. The other day, at the risk of your own life, you saved that of young Lord Fitz Barry. Now, I believe, had it been the youngest boy in the ship, you would have done the same; but Lord Fitz Barry is very anxious, as I am, that you should receive some mark to show you that your conduct is appreciated. He is not able to reward you himself, I therefore ask you whether for the future you would like to walk the quarter-deck as an officer. Through his Majesty's bounty you will have the means of doing so, and I shall have myself the satisfaction of aiding you to support your new rank. To no one else need you be indebted, and I hope in a short time that you will, by obtaining promotion, be independent of any aid beyond what you yourself can obtain."

Then turning to the midshipmen, he asked them whether they would be glad to receive the young sailor among them as a messmate. Three cheers was the answer given by the warm-hearted lads.

"We are very sure that he will not only do us credit, but gain honour for our berth," exclaimed several of them; and again they cheered their new messmate warmly.

It would be impossible to describe Denham's feelings, and perhaps few among them knew how anxious he had been to obtain the rank which was now bestowed upon him. But few days had passed since Denham had put on a uniform, and walked the quarter-deck as a midshipman, and yet in manner and appearance he was fully equal to any of his messmates. He carried on all his duties with the air of a young officer, and evidently understood them thoroughly. By his manners and conduct on all occasions, he quickly won his way in the esteem of his messmates, while his rise did not excite the envy of those below him. Ned Davis did not appear to wish to leave the position he himself occupied. Indeed, he seemed rather anxious to be an humble follower of the young midshipman than to be raised to an equality with him.

Some months had passed away, and several gallant actions had been performed by the officers and crew of the *Cynthia*, mostly in cutting-out expeditions, when Denham behaved with great gallantry. As he was much stronger, and more active than Fitz Barry, he always constituted himself the protector of the young lord whenever it was his duty to take a part in any of these expeditions.

On one occasion the frigate was off one of the French islands, and in a harbour protected by a fort on either side, several privateers and other armed vessels were discovered at anchor. As they were craft likely to do much damage to English merchant shipping, Captain Falkner resolved, though it was an undertaking of considerable risk, to cut them out. He stood off from the land toward evening, so as to give the Frenchmen the idea that he had gone away altogether. As the evening approached, however, he once more stood back for the harbour. They hoped to avoid the observations of the sentries in the forts.

Full directions were given to officers in charge of each boat. The larger vessels were to be assailed first, and two boats were to board one vessel on either quarter at the same moment. Mr. Evans had directed Denham to attack the same vessel that he proposed boarding. There were six boats, so that three privateers would be attacked simultaneously. Mr. Evans judged, by this means, that the enemy's attention being distracted, they would be prevented from coming to each other's assistance. A light breeze blew out of the harbour, which would enable them, as soon as the cables were cut, to carry the vessels off without difficulty. Not a word was spoken. The muffled oars sent forth no sound till the boats pulled up before the forts. Denham's heart beat high. He knew that he should now have an opportunity of distinguishing himself, especially under the eye of the first lieutenant, who had hitherto always proved his friend. Gradually, through the gloom of night, the masts and spars of the vessels to be attacked rose up before them. Leaving the line, he followed the boat of the first lieutenant towards a large brig which lay moored furthest out in the harbour. They were on the point of hooking on when shouts arose from her deck. They found that they were discovered; but this did not hinder them from an attempt to board. Before the Frenchmen could tell which part of the vessel they were about to

attack, they sprang up the sides of the brig, and
threw themselves on board. Part of the French
crew, having had no time to arm themselves, fled
before them to the fore-part of the vessel, where,
however, having rallied, they again rushed aft, and
a furious hand-to-hand encounter took place. Fitz
Barry had followed Denham on board, and the
young lord, pistol in hand, was advancing by the
side of his messmate. Led by Mr. Evans, the English crew dashed forward till they reached the fore-
castle, where the French, apparently determined to
resist to the last, fought bravely. Once more they
pushed the English hard. Pistol-shots were rapidly
exchanged, and the clash of cutlasses was heard,
echoed from the decks of the other vessels, which
were now also fiercely attacked. Some of the French
crew who had gone down below now appeared on
deck fully armed, and it appeared very doubtful
whether even English courage, and English determination, would succeed in overcoming the enemy.
The struggle continued. Again the enemy, led by
a huge Frenchman, who appeared to be one of
their officers, drove back the English some feet
along the deck. He had singled out Mr. Evans,
the first lieutenant, apparently with the intention
of cutting him down, being evidently himself a first-
rate swordsman. Already the English lieutenant's

guard was thrown down, and the Frenchman had lifted his cutlass and was about to bring it down on his head, when Denham sprang forward and discharged his pistol at the Frenchman. The bullet struck him on the right arm and the weapon fell to the deck. Mr. Evans, recovering his sword, gave him a thrust, which sent him backwards among his men. The fall of their leader discouraged the French, who giving way, the English found themselves in possession of the brig. The cable, as had been agreed upon, was immediately cut. -Hands were sent aloft to loose the fore-topsail, and the head of the prize coming round, she was steered out towards the mouth of the harbour.

Denham now had time to look around and ascertain what had become of Lord Fitz Barry, who was nowhere to be seen. He made inquiries of the men to learn when they had last seen him. No one knew. They had observed him on deck standing close to his brother midshipman, but after that, no one could give an account of him. Denham began to be greatly alarmed, fearing that the young lord had been thrown overboard, or that he might in the mêlée have fallen down below; but at that moment he was unable to make any further inquiries: for, as the mouth of the harbour was approached, the forts on either side opened their fire on the prize.

Although the brig offered a better mark than the boats would have done, still, as the night continued very dark, and no noise was made on board, the gunners in the forts could not ascertain in which direction to fire. The French prisoners were as eager as the English to keep quiet, because the shots which fell on board were as likely to injure them as to hurt their captors. The same reason perhaps prevented them from attempting to regain the vessel while the English were engaged in steering her out of the harbour. At length she was got clear and stood for the frigate, which now showed a bright light for her guidance; the firing having given her notice that the exploit had been attempted, although Captain Falkner, at that time, could not have told whether it had been successful or not. Mr. Evans now directed that the lantern should be lighted, in order that the French prisoners might be secured, and that it might be seen what damage had been done to the vessel. While going round the decks with a lantern, Denham discovered between the guns the form of his young messmate. A feeling of dread came over his heart. Could he have been killed and fallen down there? He lifted him up, and anxiously examined his countenance.

"Speak, speak, Fitz Barry," he exclaimed eagerly.

"Do tell me if you are hurt, or where you have been wounded."

"Yes, I am hurt, somewhat badly I am afraid," answered Fitz Barry, at length, in a faint voice. "I was thrown down there by the Frenchmen we were fighting with, and I was unable after that to move. I did not like to cry out, remembering that we were passing the fort; and soon after that, I suppose, I fainted."

"I thank Heaven that you are able to speak thus," said Denham, "and we shall soon be on board the frigate, and the doctor will look to your hurts."

Mr. Evans had the satisfaction of observing two other vessels following him out of the harbour, while a bright light which burst forth some way up it showed that the other boats had had time to set some merchantmen on fire. War is a fearful thing at all times, but more sad even is it when it compels the destruction of private property.

No one, however, would have objected to the destruction of privateers. It is pretty well agreed they partake more of the character of pirates than honourable combatants; their only object is to rob the merchantmen of the enemy, so as to become themselves the possessors of their rich freight. They do not fight for honour or glory, and they care as little for the good of their country. It is true, however, that the privateers, by injuring the commerce of the enemy, frequently make that enemy more anxious to come to terms, but in most cases both parties are engaged in the same infamous system; both equally suffer, and both increase the horrors and sufferings of warfare.

When morning dawned, the prizes were found collected round the frigate. Denham's first care was to get the wounded young midshipman conveyed on board, that the doctor might immediately look at his hurts. He did not attempt to conceal his sorrow and anxiety. He seemed to feel that it was from his carelessness by some means or other the poor lad had been injured. Mr. Evans had a very different account to give of him, however, and at once generously informed Captain Falkner that it was to his nerve and courage that he himself owed his life.

The Frenchmen were removed on board the frigate, and an English prize crew being placed on board each of the prizes, they and their captor steered a course for Jamaica. Captain Falkner offered to place Denham in command of one of the prizes, but his anxiety for young Lord Fitz Barry made him beg that he might be allowed to remain on board the frigate.

A considerable time had passed since the arrival

of the *Cynthia* on the station. A season dreaded by all navigators of those seas was now approaching— the hurricane season. Fearful is the devastation often produced on shore and on the ocean at that period. Not many years before several line of battle ships and other vessels had either foundered with their crews, or had been driven on shore, where the larger number of the men belonging to them had perished. Captain Falkner was anxious, therefore, to get back without delay to Port Royal harbour. They were, however, within a couple of days' sail of Jamaica when the frigate was becalmed; during the middle of the day, although a thick mist overspread the sky and hid the rays of the sun, the heat was excessive. Below the ship was like an oven, on deck not a breath of air was to be obtained. The men in their white shirts and trousers, moved languidly about, literally gasping for breath. The sails hung uselessly down against the masts, and the frigate's head went slowly round and round, now pointing in one direction and now in another, though it was difficult to say by what power she was moved.

The heat affected young Barry greatly. Denham sat by his side whenever he could leave his duty on deck, anxiously watching his friend. Ned Davis also came where the wounded midshipman lay and begged that he might be allowed to take Denham's place by his side. It was curious to observe how Denham had won the lad's affection and admiration. There seemed to have been no previous tie between them; they had met, it was understood, for the first time as shipmates on board the merchantman from which they had volunteered, and it was possible neither of them knew much about each other's previous history. No nurse could have administered the medicine prescribed by the doctor with more care and regularity than did Denham and his volunteer assistant.

"I hope I shall not die," said Fitz Barry, taking his hand, "I want very much again to see my kind father, and my dear little sister Nora, whom I have told you about, and my cousin Sophy; and do you know, I think I shall see them before long. The last letter I got from home, my father told me that he expected to obtain an appointment as governor of one of the West India islands. It is not a thing he would have accepted under ordinary circumstances, but the truth is, I suspect that it has been very expensive living in Ireland for the last few years, and he thinks it will be wise to economize a little. I do not know much about these things; he has supplied me liberally with money, and that is all I have to think about. I believe Captain Falkner expects to see him out here, for he spoke of him the other day, and you know, I do not mind telling you, that I believe our skipper is going to marry Sophy one of these days. I am sure you would like her and my sister if you ever were to see them. I do not know which you would like best. Nora is a very sweet little girl, or at least, by the by, she must have grown since I left home a good deal. She is older than I am rather, and so fair and gentle, but she has not the spirit of Sophy, or her cleverness; Sophy is a wonderfully clever girl, she draws so well. She used to make such beautiful portraits of people. However, I must not praise her too much, or you may possibly be disappointed."

Denham told Fitz Barry that he should very much like to be introduced to his relations; "but you know," he observed, "I am afraid they will think very little of me when they hear that I was a boy before the mast. I tell you, Barry, we are messmates, and therefore it is right that we should be equal; but from what I have learned that will not do on shore; people think there a good deal about the difference of rank, and if I was to make my appearance among some of those great people, they might treat me in a way that I should not at all like. I have become very proud, I am afraid, since I have been placed on the quarter-deck, not for myself, perhaps, so much, but for the honour of the rank I bear, for the cloth, even though I am as yet but a midshipman.

Fitz Barry smiled faintly, and answered languidly, " O, no fear of that; I am sure my father and Sophy are not a bit proud; and as to Nora, I don't think she has a particle of that sort of thing in her; so when they come, you must promise to let me make you known to them."

Denham did not wish to appear to refuse his friend, at the same time he resolved not in any way to push himself forward. The conversation appeared to be doing Fitz Barry good. Though severely injured by the thrust of a pike in his side, and a blow on his head, which had knocked him down, the doctor assured Captain Falkner that he did not consider the boy's life in any peril.

Captain Falkner and Mr. Evans were holding a consultation on the deck. Directly afterwards the latter shouted, " All hands on deck, and shorten sail."

The men came rapidly tumbling up from below, some looking round astonished at hearing the order, seeing that the dog-vane was still hanging up and down the rigging. They sprang immediately aloft and the sails were rapidly furled.

" Starboard the helm," shouted the lieutenant, gazing round the horizon as he did so. " Closely reef the fore-topsail," he added; "man the fore-top-sail braces."

The fore-topsail was the only sail now set. At that instant a dark line was seen sweeping rapidly over the water. As it approached it seemed to rise as it were above the surface and break into feathery-topped seas. On it came. A fierce blast struck the ship on the starboard side, and she heeled over till the guns on the other side dipped in the water. Quickly recovering herself, however, the fore-topsail being braced sharp up, her head "paid off" before the wind. Once more the topsail was squared, and away she flew before the wind. Wonderful was the change. A few minutes before the sea appeared as smooth as polished glass; now it was one mass of broken waves, leaping and dancing madly around. On flew the frigate. The captain and master went below to examine the chart, and to see the direction in which she was driving. It might have availed them little, however, for it seemed impossible to steer her during the fierce gale which blew in any other direction than directly before it. On she went, the wind rapidly increasing; the seas rose higher and higher, and in a short time a fierce hurricane was raging. The stern-ports were secured, the hatches were battened down, and every preparation made to prepare her for the worst. Probably in a short time she would not be able to run before the gale.

"We have a clear sea before us," observed the captain to the master, as they leaned over the chart to which the former pointed; "that, unless the wind shifts, gives us a better hope of escaping. The ship, too, considering the number of years she has been at sea, is in a good state, and I do not think we need fear her springing a leak."

The master seemed to agree with Captain Falkner and once more they together returned on deck.

Denham, all the time he had been in the West Indies, had never encountered such a hurricane. He gazed with admiration, allied with awe, on the vast seas which now rose up on every side around them. The stout frigate was tossed about as if she had been a cockle-shell, yet on she flew unharmed, now sinking into the deep trough of the sea, now rising to the summit of a mountainous billow.

"I wish Fitz Barry had been able to come on deck; he was saying the other day how he should like to witness a real hurricane," he observed to one of his messmates,

"Oh, Fitz Barry fancies a great many things; but I wonder whether he would like the reality of this," was the answer.

"He has as brave and true a heart as ever lived,"

answered Denham warmly. "Depend upon it, there is more in him than some of you suppose."

"Considering that he is a lord he is all very well," answered Denham's messmate. "In my opinion he has been over-petted and spoiled."

The frigate flew onward on her course. Provided none of her rigging gave way, and no leak was sprung, it seemed probable she would escape without any misfortune. But everything at the present moment appeared to depend upon the rigging and the sea-worthiness of her hull. Still the captain and his officers often looked anxiously around. The fury of the hurricane was evidently increasing; it had not yet got to its height. The fore-topsail had hitherto stood, but as it tugged and tugged away it seemed as if it would fly from the bolt-ropes. The first lieutenant anxiously watched it. Should it be carried away it was scarcely possible that another could be set, and though the ship might still scud under bare poles, there was a great risk of her broaching to, and if so, the seas breaking over her sides might disable her completely. Suddenly there was a loud clap like that of thunder, and what looked for the moment like a white cloud was seen carried away before the blast. It was the fore-topsail which had been blown from the bolt-ropes. The few shreds that remained were quickly wrapped round and round the yard, whence it would be no easy matter to cut them. Still the ship went on under bare poles. At length night approached, and as darkness came on the danger was greatly increased. Even flying as she was before the wind those on board could scarcely keep their feet, and more than one remarked, "What must it be for poor people on shore? Why, half the plantations in Jamaica will be carried away."

"Worse still for those at sea who are on a lee shore," observed Mr. Evans. "Let us pray that we may not find ourselves in that position."

The men generally behaved very well during the awful scene, but there were some skulkers who went below to hide themselves away. Among them was John Higson. He had been bold and boasting in fine weather, but he now showed himself to be the coward he really was. The second lieutenant, going his rounds on the lower deck, found him stowed away, hoping to be out of sight, with two or three others of the same character. He instantly ordered them up on deck to do their duty, though they very unwillingly obeyed.

"Do you think that the hurricane will soon be over, master?" asked Captain Falkner.

"Not for some hours, I fear," answered the master. "I have known such a one as this last twenty-four hours at least, and wonderful was the mischief it did in that time. However, as long as we can keep her from broaching to, we shall do well enough."

While he was speaking there was a fearful crash. Loud shrieks were heard. The main-yard had been carried from the slings, as it fell crushing several persons who stood below it.

Several of their messmates rushed to the spot to aid them. Four or five were killed, and others were sadly mangled. Still the frigate drove on.

"A sail ahead," shouted the look-out.

Glasses were turned in that direction, and a large ship was seen now sinking in the trough of the sea, now rising to the summit of the waves.

"She is a line-of-battle ship, I think," said Mr. Evans to Captain Falkner, "and from the way she is rolling I fear she is in a bad condition."

The blast which had carried away the frigate's main-yard appeared to be the last effort of the hurricane. The wind began to subside almost as rapidly as it commenced. In a short time, although the sea continued raging fiercely, the wind had dropped to a moderate gale. The wreck of the yard having been cleared away, sail was once more made on the frigate, and she steered towards the line-of-battle ship.

As she approached every indication was observed that she had suffered fearfully in the hurricane. Her ensign was hoisted reversed. The bowsprit and fore topmast were gone, as was the mizen topmast, while it seemed as if in an instant the main topmast would follow the other masts. All the quarter boats seemed to have been carried away, and as the frigate drew nearer a signal was hoisted, which, on being interpreted, was—

"Come as close as you can; we have passengers on board, and are expecting every instant to go down."

The roughness of the sea rendered the passage of boats between the two ships very dangerous. Still Captain Falkner determined to risk them with the ordinary boats' crews; though, in such cases, volunteers are often called for. He immediately answered the signal,—"We will send boats; be prepared to lower your passengers into them."

The first and second lieutenants went each to take command of a boat, and Denham was directed to take charge of one in the place of one of the other officers who was ill. While the boats were passing between the two ships, two men were employed in each to bale out the water which broke into them.

CHAPTER IX.

WE must now take a glance at the events which had occurred on the shores of Kilfinnan Bay since young Dermot O'Neil left his mother's cottage.

The Earl had continued his course of hospitality, or extravagance, as it should more correctly have been denominated, such as was too much the custom among most Irish gentlemen of those days, declaring that although his affairs at that time were in a rather embarrassed condition, he could not afford to commence a system of economy. His table, as usual, was amply spread, and the members of the neighbouring hunt pretty frequently in the season collected at the castle, which during the summer months was seldom otherwise than full of guests. Lady Nora, who was now growing into a beautiful young woman, saw with regret the lavish expenditure in which her father indulged, knowing very well from what she had heard, that it was more than his income could afford; still he always contrived to supply Barry amply with money, and Nora was allowed every luxury she could wish for. Her tastes, however, were very simple, though in her visits with her father to the gay Irish capital, she was compelled, much against her will, to mix in its frivolous society, when at the castle she was content to take her usual rides about the country, often with no other attendant than a young lad on a rough pony to hold her horse, should she wish to alight.

Lady Sophy still continued to be for the greater part of the year her constant companion. Occasionally, they looked in upon Mr. Jamieson, the minister, and his blind niece, Miss O'Reilly. They did not forget either the old fish-wife, the Widow O'Neil. Whenever they saw her, they did not fail to inquire about her son; but she shook her head, with a melancholy look.

"He will come back some day, I know he will. He promised me he would; but he does not write to me—he sends me no messages. Perhaps, as he knows I cannot read, he thinks it will be no use writing; but, oh, he loves me dearly; and it is for no want of love he does not write. He will come back to me, dear young ladies, some day; and, oh, . with what pride I shall have to bring him to you. He will be a fine, strong lad by that time. Maybe you would not know him. He must be altered greatly since the day you took his picture, when he was a young fisher-boy."

Mr. Jamieson, however, was more surprised than any one else at not hearing from Dermot. He had been fully prepared for Dermot's going away, but he did not for one moment suppose, from what he knew of the lad, that he would not have kept up a correspondence with his friends at home. Still, he had received no letter, and had seen none from him to any one else, since the epistle brought by mad Kathleen a few days after his departure. Had it not been for this, he would have supposed he had met with some foul treatment from the rebels, or that some fearful accident had befallen him. Still, whenever Miss O'Reilly spoke to the widow, the old woman expressed her firm belief that Dermot was living, and would most assuredly come back to her. That thought seemed to keep her alive, and to give her strength of mind and body to go through her accustomed duties. Sometimes, however, it appeared to the blind lady, when she listened to the old woman, that her mind was not altogether right, for she spoke of strange things she had seen and done in her youth, the meaning of which Miss O'Reilly could not comprehend. She could not, however, listen to her speaking of Dermot without feeling touched by the deep love which formed, as it were, a part of her being, for her young son. There was one person however, who could have given more information about the matter than anybody else, if he had chosen—that was Father O'Rourke. For purposes best known to himself, he had gained an undue influence over the authorities at the post-office, and thus he had the means of examining any letters which he thought it worth his while to look into. Though such a thing might be impossible at the present day, at that time it was easy of execution.

On one occasion when he was glancing over the letters, he found one, the superscription of which he examined carefully. Taking it aside, he broke it open.

"O, and so you recommend your mother to go and listen to the counsels of the heretic minister. Is that your idea, Master Dermot?" he exclaimed to himself. "We shall see how that is carried out. And you declare your love to her; and you vow that, Heaven protecting you, you will return, you trust, with wealth in your pockets, and that you will place her above want; and you hope that she has accepted the faith which you yourself now profess." The priest literally ground his teeth with anger. "You warn her to beware of one, your right and lawful spiritual adviser, do you? She shall, at all events, remain faithful to the true Church. I will take care she does not set eyes upon that heretic, Mr. Jamieson. Well! well! you think yourself clever at forming a plot; but I will soon show you that I can counteract it. You tell her that you will write to Mr. Jamieson, do you? I will take care he does not get a letter either. Is my authority thus to be set at defiance by a—well, no matter what you are. I know more of your affairs than you do, or than your poor, ignorant, half-witted mother does herself; though she is cunning enough to hide away those documents which would, could I find them, place you and her, and some other persons, too, entirely in my power. I'll find them still, however, some day; but that English minister, by teaching you to read, has made the management of the business far more difficult than it would have been. However, I'll not be baulked. We see what folly it is to let any but the priests and the wealthy classes to be taught to read. They would be managed ten times more easily than they will be in a short time, if this sort of thing goes on. Ah! I was thinking of that, lad. You may be clever, Master Dermot, but I will prove to you that there is one here cleverer than yourself. Did I know where to write you, I would soon prove that; but, ere long, I doubt not that another of your letters will come under my inspection, and then I will quickly settle the matter."

Such were the thoughts—for they were not words—which passed through the mind of the Romish priest. Poor Dermot! little did he think what was to be the fate of the loving letter he had written to his mother, the first he had had the opportunity of inditing after he had left the shores of England.

Days, and weeks, and months passed on and the widow had heard nothing of her son. The priest, however, after watching month after month, at length found a letter, which seemed to give him infinite satisfaction. Its contents need not be revealed; but Father O'Rourke had at length found the means, so it appeared from his ejaculations, by which he could communicate with Dermot.

The day arrived when the Earl and his family were to quit Kilfinnan Castle. Their neighbours and friends, and the surrounding peasantry, turned out to bid them farewell.

Numberless were the expressions of affection and regard given utterance to, as persons of all ranks came forward to pay their adieux to the Earl, but more especially to Lady Nora, and her cousin, Lady Sophy. Lady Nora shed many tears. She was bidding farewell to the spot she loved, where the gentle mother whom she could just recollect had breathed her last, and round which were centred all the pleasant recollections of her youth. She was going to a strange land, to a country where she had heard of pestilence stalking forth in the noonday, and her heart sank within her, to think of the dangers to which her father might be exposed. Yet one thing consoled her—she hoped there to meet her brother, who was still, she knew, on the station, though a report had come that the ship was about to leave it.

Among the guests were Mr. Jamieson and his blind niece. The Earl shook them warmly by the hand. "If anything happens to me, Jamieson, remember I charge you to look after my young boy. He is a good and a brave youth, but he requires a friend; and Nora, Miss O'Reilly, I would rather you had charge of her than anybody on earth, and yet I am afraid she is growing too old to be under the guidance of any one; I suspect, too, she could only be led by the hand of love. She is a dear, sweet girl, and I often think if I am taken away, what is to become of her in this cruel world. Jamieson, I need not conceal from you that I believe my affairs are cruelly disarranged. It is hard work, you know, to get in the rents, and of late years, my steward has told me, and I believe him, that it has been harder than ever. I do not like to press the tenants; I never yet had a distress executed, but without it I am afraid there are some of them who will never be ready to pay."

"Trust to our merciful Father, my dear lord," answered Mr. Jamieson. "Do your duty and try to serve Him. There is no use denying it, you are not free from blame for this state of things, and I am very certain, that may be said of the greater number of landlords of this country, so the only advice I can give is to retrench for the future, and when you come back, to set manfully to work to get your affairs in order."

"Thank you, Jamieson, I think your advice is excellent," said the good-natured Earl; "farewell, I will try and follow it out."

Numbers of gentlemen, and farmers, and peasantry, accompanied the carriages of the Earl and his party on horseback, as they took their way towards Cork, whence the line-of-battle ship which was to take them on board was to sail.

CHAPTER X.

WE must now return to the West Indies. At length the frigate's boat reached the line-of-battle ship. Numbers of persons were looking through the ports. Denham's boat was one of the first on the starboard side.

"We must lower the ladies first," said a voice from the entrance port. "Stand ready to receive them, there is no time to be lost."

"All right," answered Denham, looking up.

At the same moment a chair was lowered from the entrance port. In an instant, the occupant, a young lady, was released and placed in the boat. Again the chair ascended, and another was lowered in the same way. Denham, giving one glance at her countenance, saw that she was fair and young, and having placed her in security, he had to attend to those who followed. Three others were immediately lowered together.

"Now, my lord," said the voice of an officer, "you must go into the boat."

"No, no, not till all the females are out of the ship," was the answer.

"They are being placed in the other boats; there is no time to be lost; let me entreat you to descend," said the officer.

"Well, if I must go, I will obey you," answered the nobleman who had been addressed, "but I trust all on board here will escape." As he spoke he was lowered down into the boat.

"Come, some of you youngsters, follow him," said a voice; "there will be but little time for the boats to make many trips between the ships; come, I say, obey orders." At that moment five or six young midshipmen came tumbling into the boat, which now being more than sufficiently laden, pulled back to the frigate.

"I am very glad you are here, Lord Kilfinnan," said one of them, "and I hope Lady Nora has not been very much frightened. It has been terrible work though, and I am afraid the old bark will not swim much longer."

"Give way, my lads, give way," shouted Denham to his crew; "we must be back before the ship sinks, or I am afraid many a fine fellow will lose his life."

The men rowed as hard as they could, and in a short time they again reached the frigate. No time was lost in handing up those on board.

FOUNDERING OF THE VESSEL.

"Whom have we here?" asked Captain Falkner.

"Lord Kilfinnan, and his daughter, and niece," answered Denham, "and several other ladies and midshipmen. But we must be back to the ship, for they expect every moment that she will go down."

"Mr. Evans," said Captain Falkner, "we must get out the launch and pinnace; the sea is calm enough now to allow us to do so."

While the rest of the boats already in the water, having put those they carried on board the frigate, pulled back to the line-of-battle ship, the larger boats were cleared and hoisted out, though not without the risk of being stove alongside. The smaller boats had already made a couple of trips before they were ready to shove off for the ship. At length away they pulled, but as they reached the side of the ship the cry arose, "She is sinking—she is sinking."

Numbers of the brave fellows who had hitherto preserved their discipline now threw themselves headlong into the boats. The marines still remained drawn up on deck, where they had been posted to preserve order. Already all the boats were full almost to sinking, and with their living freight they proceeded slowly back to the frigate; she, meantime, had been drawing nearer and nearer the ship. Still the vast fabric floated above the waves; many yet remained on board. The gallant marines stood as if on parade; the officers who had refused to quit the ship clustered on the quarter-deck. Who could have believed that all knew that in not many moments the planks on which they stood would be engulfed by the waves, yet so it was; British discipline triumphed above the fear of death.

With frantic haste the men in the boats sprang up the side of the frigate, in order that they might speedily return to the ship. Already they were half way between the two vessels when the line-of-battle ship lifted high her bows above the water, then down she plunged, still with many human beings standing on her decks, numbers, alas! sinking never to rise again. The boats dashed forward into the midst of the vortex caused by her sudden descent. It seemed for a moment that they also would be drawn down by it. On every side were human beings, some already dead it seemed, others crying out for assistance, while some, refusing to express their fears, were striking out boldly for life towards the boats. There were but few, alas! of the brave marines; it seemed as if they must have grasped their muskets to the last, and gone down with those heavy weights in their hands. Eagerly the boats pulled backwards and forwards among their fellow creatures still floating in the water; as rapidly as they could they pulled them on board, till at length all who appeared alive were rescued. But it was too certain that a very large number both of officers and crew had gone down in the sinking ship.

Such has been the fate of many a gallant crew in every part of the world. The survivors were carried on board the frigate, and treated with every kindness which the officers and crew were able to bestow. The gallant captain of the line-of-battle ship, two of his lieutenants, and several inferior officers, with nearly half of the marines, were lost. The frigate having once more hoisted her boats on board, made sail for Port Royal.

The Earl of Kilfinnan, on discovering the name of the frigate by which he had been rescued, inquired at once for his son. His cheek turned pale when he did not see him with the midshipmen of the ship. The truth was told him that he had been wounded.

"But he is doing well, my lord," said the surgeon to whom he was speaking; "before long I hope he will be able to return to his duty."

Lady Sophy could with difficulty conceal her feelings when she heard that Captain Falkner commanded the ship to which she had been conveyed, while it would be impossible to describe the satisfaction which she experienced. Nora insisted at once on going down and seeing poor Barry, who was still unable to leave his cot. At first he would scarcely believe who it was who stood before him, and for some time he fancied himself in a dream, and asked whether he had not got an increase of fever.

"O no, dear Barry," answered Nora, "in a short time you will be well, and it will be a good excuse for you to come and live on .shore with us. I hear the place we are going to is very beautiful, high up on the side of a mountain, far above all the mists and vapours which bring the yellow fever into this part of the world. And papa, you know, is to be the governor, so that he will not feel the change from Kilfinnan Castle so great as he might have done, for, of course, the people will treat him with great respect, and that you know he likes, although he does not talk about it; and we shall have horses to ride about the country, and plenty of people to attend upon us, and there are a number of curious fruits and animals, and creatures of all sorts which we shall have to see. Now I fully expect to be very interested, and so must you be, Barry, and I daresay Captain Falkner will occasionally come and see dear Sophy, and that will make her very happy."

Thus Nora ran on in her light-hearted way, anxious to raise her brother's spirits. She felt somewhat sad, however, when she looked at him, for the bright glow in his cheeks was gone, and he looked so pale and thin that she began to fear he might be worse than the doctor said he was. After the hurricane the frigate had a fine passage to Port Royal. There, having landed all her supernumeraries by the orders of the admiral, she once more sailed to carry the Earl to his destination. He was received with the usual honours of a Lieutenant-Governor, and carriages were in waiting to convey him to his country seat, on the side of the mountain which had been described by Nora. It was a lovely spot, with streams gushing down from the side of the steep heights above the house, while the wide terrace in front afforded ample room for exercise.

Far below the white buildings of the chief town was to be seen the intermediate country, covered with the richest tropical vegetation, while in the distance was the deep blue sea, dotted here and there with the white sails of vessels of various sizes. Barry of course had leave to accompany his father on shore, and he begged that his friend Denham should be allowed to pay them a visit.

"He has been watching over me so carefully while I was sick on board, that it would seem ungrateful in me if I did not ask him to come with

11

us. Besides, he is so excellent a fellow—so brave, and daring, and generous. I do not mean to say in the matter of money, because he has none of that, for he was only a few years ago placed on the quarter-deck, but I mean in his behaviour. He never takes offence, and never thinks ill of anybody, and he will never allow any of the younger fellows to be bullied by the elder, whom he is strong enough to keep in order, and there are not many who can beat him in any way."

The next day, accordingly, the Earl wrote a note to Captain Falkner, requesting that Mr. Denham might be allowed to pay him a visit. Captain Falkner, who had been much pleased with the conduct of the young midshipman, was glad to accede to the Earl's request, and told Denham to prepare for a visit on shore. Denham made some excuse with regard to his outfit.

"Oh, I will settle all that," answered the captain kindly, "I must be your banker, remember, and just go on shore at once, and we will get Mr. Truefit to rig you out in the course of a few hours. They do not take long to do that sort of thing out here."

Thus all difficulties were overcome, and the following day Denham found himself on his way to the new Governor's house.

CHAPTER XI.

A S soon as Denham approached the Government house, Barry, who had seen him from the window, hastened forward to meet him, and after the first greetings, said that he must introduce him at once to the Earl, and his sister, and cousin.

"You will like the girls," he whispered to Denham, "you must be entirely at your ease with them, remember, they are not fine, they have no nonsense about them, just as girls should be; if they were otherwise, I, for one, would not own them. I have no idea of girls giving themselves airs."

Saying this, Barry led Denham into the drawing-room. The young midshipman seemed to have the habit of blushing, for in spite of all he could do, the colour mounted to his cheeks when he made his bow, a very graceful one, by-the-by, to the two young ladies. He conversed with ease, but the subjects of his conversation, as far as he selected them, were entirely confined to the scenes he had witnessed in the West Indies, or to a few books which he had the opportunity of reading since he had been on board the frigate. As to England, or any other part of the world, he seemed to know nothing whatever, as far at least as his own experience went. He did not speak either of his family or of any friend he possessed, and they soon came to the conclusion that he was either a foundling or an orphan, without any relation whom he wished to own. Still they were very much pleased with his general conversation.

Captain Falkner, in the evening, came up to the Government house, and he then said that the Admiral had directed him to take a cruise for a few weeks, and that, at the end of the time, he would come back for his midshipmen. He was able, however, to remain at anchor two or three days, and, as will be supposed, he spent most of his time on shore in Lady Sophy's company. No one could watch the two without agreeing that they were admirably matched. She, gentle and intelligent, and affectionate; he, frank and brave, and open-hearted in his manner and bearing. He was known, too, as a just, brave, high-spirited officer, and a very first-rate seaman, and more than that, to be a God-fearing religious man.

The two midshipmen, it should have been remarked, when last at Jamaica, had passed their examination, which gave them the rank of masters' mates, as they were called in those days. They had been for some time on shore when, a mail arriving, the Earl presented Denham with a long official-looking letter. Denham eagerly opened it. His heart beat quicker than usual; the colour rose to his cheeks, and his eyes beamed with pleasure, for he found that the document announced his being raised to the rank of lieutenant. The Earl seemed to be aware of the fact, and soon after addressed him as "Lieutenant Denham."

"But has not Barry also got his promotion?" asked Denham, looking at his friend.

"Yes," answered Barry, "I am a lieutenant too, but I do not feel as you do, because I am sure I have not deserved it. You have done all sorts of gallant things, and I have done nothing."

The Earl laughed.

"Well," he said, "provided those who deserve promotion obtain it, the Admiralty do not object to raise a few who have less to boast of."

"But I am sure you would have done all sorts of gallant things if you had had the opportunity," said Lady Nora, turning to her brother with a smile.

"I hope this will not remove me from the *Cynthia*," said Denham; "I should indeed be sorry to quit Captain Falkner and my old shipmates."

"I think not," answered the Earl. "From what I hear from the Admiral who writes to me on the subject, the first lieutenant of the *Cynthia* has been promoted, and another officer has left the ship, so that you two will get the vacancies. I hope in the course of another month or so she will return from Jamaica, and that Barry will rejoin her with renewed health."

The father's hope buoyed him up, while Denham could not help acknowledging that he saw his friend every day growing weaker and weaker. It was evident that the injuries he had received in the cutting-out expedition had been more severe than had been supposed, and that his system had received a shock from which it had never recovered. Nora, too, was scarcely aware of the danger of her brother. Lady Sophy, perhaps, had suspected it, but could not bring herself to speak of it to her cousin. Barry himself declared that he felt better every day, though he showed, by his disinclination to take exercise, that he was much weaker than he was ready to acknowledge.

At length the frigate came back, and the two young lieutenants rejoined her. When, however, Lord Barry came on board, the surgeon kindly told him that he thought he would be better off by remaining on shore a little longer with his father.

The surgeon saw that a great change had taken place in him.

Barry declared he was fully capable of doing his duty, but the surgeon persisted in advising him to return home.

"I am sure a little more rest will do you good," said Captain Falkner, looking at him compassionately; "we will manage to have your duty done on board, and we must hope that in a short time you will be sufficiently recovered to resume it yourself."

The Earl was somewhat surprised at seeing Barry return, but Captain Falkner, who accompanied him, endeavoured to tranquilize his mind; and though he could not honestly say his son would recover, he remarked that youth and a good constitution often enable persons to gain strength when otherwise it might be hopeless.

The *Cynthia* was ordered to cruise about the Windward Islands; a dangerous locality, but where she would have many places to visit. Captain Falkner observed that he should frequently have to call off the island, and that he hoped to see the Earl and his family whenever he did so.

It would be difficult to describe the beautiful scenery of the island now placed under the government of the Earl. The ground is broken into hills and valleys, and here and there lofty mountains rise, towering high up into the blue sky. Good roads, however, are cut across the island in every direction, and thus not only were the young ladies able to drive about, but they also had the pleasure of taking long rides to many scenes of beauty, accompanied by Barry, who, though he did not appear to recover his strength, was still able to sit on horseback. A number of planters were settled about the island, many of whom were men of education, and all were glad to offer hospitality to the Earl and his sick son. The Earl hoped by travelling about, and by amusing Barry's mind, to assist in the restoration of his health. They had on one occasion gone to a planter's house at the back of the island, a day's journey from the Earl's country residence, and situated near the sea.

The spot was a very beautiful one. In the background rose ranges of mountains, feathered to their very summits with green foliage. On one side of the grounds were plantations of coffee and sugar. The sandy beach stretched like a line of silver along the edge of the blue water, fringing the cane-fields, which formed a broad expanse of vivid green behind them. Along the coast were lovely little coves and bays, enlivened by neatly laid out mansions of the planters, while numerous fishing

and passage boats, with their raking masts and lat-
teen sails, added life and animation to the scene.
A bright and sparkling stream, which found its way
down from the mountains above, passed through the
plantation, and added much to the refreshing cool-
ness of the scene in that warm climate. A broad
verandah ran round the house, on one side of which
or the other shade could be obtained at all times of
the day. A couple of days had been spent very
pleasantly at this abode, when one evening, just as
the sun was about to sink through a rain cloud into
the distant horizon, an old white-headed slave came
hurriedly into the presence of his master.

" What is the matter, Cæsar," asked Mr. Jefferson,
the planter. The old man shook his head.

" Very bad, very bad."

" Speak, boy; have you lost your wits ?" exclaimed the planter impatiently.

" No, massa ; but me hear there come one hundred Caribs and many white men, and a whole lot
of negroes, to burn the house this night and the
plantations ; and they swear that they will kill all
the people."

At first the planter was inclined to laugh at this
information, so indeed was the Earl ; but, on a further examination, the statements of the negro were
so clear—and he was so well able to explain how

he obtained his knowledge—that they began to think more seriously.

"It is too late now," observed the planter, "for your lordship to attempt to return to the town; indeed, you would be very likely to fall in with these rebels; but I have several trusty slaves on the estate who I am sure would be ready to lay down their lives for my sake. I will send Cæsar to summon them into the house, and as I know that we can make a better stand here than at the residences of any of the other planters, I shall be able to persuade several of them to come here with their families, and assist in the defence of the place."

"In the mean time we must send off for assistance," observed the Earl; "I am perfectly ready to agree to your proposition; indeed, I should be very unwilling to attempt to travel with my two young ladies and son at this hour; besides which we should probably be watched, and if we were so, we should eventually be captured by these people. But what could have caused them to think of rebelling?"

" Probably, my lord, emissaries from France have landed on the island, and also there are several discontented settlers of other nations, besides Caribs and blacks, who are always ready for a disturbance, in the hopes of gaining something during it."

"However," observed the Earl, who in his youth

had been a soldier, "we must make preparations for defending the place; I have had a little experience of that sort of thing in Ireland, and I suspect there is not much difference between the characters we shall have to deal with and those I have been accustomed to in my native country."

Mr. Jefferson, as he had proposed, immediately sent out three of his most trusty household servants, with notes to the neighbouring planters, inviting them to take refuge in his house, while the other servants of the establishment were at once ordered to come in. A number of trees from the neighbouring woods were forthwith cut down and brought into the house, to assist in barricading the windows and doors. Every available board, tops of tables and chests were broken up to close all the entrances, loop-holes being cut in them through which muskets could be fired at the advancing foe. Neither Lady Sophy nor Lady Nora seemed much alarmed at seeing the preparations.

"It reminds me very much of our younger days," observed Lady Sophy to her cousin. "You remember what work there was in defending the old castle, though that appeared to us to be a far better place to defend than this is. Still as our friends do not appear to be alarmed I do not see why we should be."

Lord Barry seemed aroused by the exertions he was called on to make, and set to work with zeal in assisting in fortifying the house; all languor had disappeared, and he was now full of animation. In a short time the gentlemen who had been summoned arrived at the house. Most of them came attended by servants well armed, and several who had families brought them also, not forgetting to bring, at the same time, a supply of provisions. They all knew that some time might elapse before they could get assistance. Indeed, if, as was not improbable, there was a general rising of the Caribs and blacks on the island, the small number of troops stationed in the garrison would be fully occupied in attempting to put them down, and perhaps none could be spared to come to their relief. None of the party, however, appeared alarmed. They held the people it was expected would attack them in too much contempt not to feel perfectly secure with the preparations they had had time to make. The Earl's chief annoyance arose in not having himself received information of the intended rising, as, of course, he felt himself responsible for the well-being of the country. He, however, took care to exhibit no doubt or hesitation, and did his utmost to keep up the resolution of those collected about him. It should have been said, that the day after the *Cynthia* left the harbour, a boat with several men had contrived to escape from the side of the ship.

It happened in the following manner. During the latter part of the middle watch, while the night was excessively dark, there was a shout of a man overboard. The wind was light. A boat was ordered to be lowered, and to pull in the direction in which the man was supposed to have floated. There was no cry, however, though a splash was heard, and fears were therefore entertained that he had sunk, or had become the prey of a shark; there was far more confusion than usual on board at the time, and several voices were heard exclaiming, that he was crying out, and that the sound came from a different direction to that in which the first boat had gone. Without waiting for orders, another boat was immediately lowered; it was known that several men had jumped into her, and shoved off without an officer; when it was, as on the present occasion, a matter of life and death, this was not of much consequence. Away the boat pulled from the ship, and no officer took upon himself to call her back. At length, however, it appearing certain that the man must have sunk, or, what was too likely, been carried off by a shark, the boats were recalled on board. One only returned. In vain the other was summoned. No answer was made to the repeated calls of the boatswain. A gun was fired; still, after waiting a certain time, the boat did not return. It was strange that no one could tell in which direction she had gone. It was scarcely possible that any accident could have happened to her; for, even if she had filled with water, the men in her would certainly have cried out. The ship at the time was supposed to be about five or six leagues from the land, which had been seen at sundown over the weather quarter. Since then the wind had been very light, and the ship had made but little way. The natural conclusion to which Captain Falkner came was, the boat must have pulled on shore, and made several tacks in that direction. A strong gale, however, coming on in a short time, he was unable to beat up to the island; and after making an attempt for some hours in vain, having despatches on board, he was obliged to bear up for his destination. He intended, however, on his return to make inquiries for the boat, in case she should have reached the shore. Now, it happened that the mutineer, Higson, had managed to win over six of the men to assist him in escaping from the ship. At his suggestion a log had been thrown into the water, and the cry was raised that a man was overboard. This done, he had no great difficulty in leaving the ship. While in harbour he had had frequent communications with various persons disaffected to the Government. He had by chance fallen in with one of them when he was on shore, and this led to his communication with others. Believing that the larger portion of the population would join in a rebellion, he entertained the idea of making himself of some importance in the country, fully believing that assistance would be gained from the French or Dutch, and that the people might make themselves independent of England. With this object in view, he determined to leave the ship.

His success was complete, and he managed before dawn to land safely on the island. Here the boat was broken up, and a cave by the shore being found, the fragments were piled up in it and completely consumed; thus he hoped all trace of his landing was lost. He had some difficulty in finding the people with whom he had before communicated, but at length they met, and he at once entered seriously into the plans which had been proposed for overpowering the British troops, and taking possession of the country. He knew where the Earl was living, and entertaining a personal grudge against him for the part he had played in sending him on board a man-of-war, he resolved on wreaking his vengeance in the first place on his head. On visiting the governor's country house he discovered that the Earl had gone to the plantation of Mr. Jefferson, and he immediately determined, with such aid as he could collect, to attack it, in the hopes of at once either capturing the Earl or destroying him and his family.

Happily, having to deal with people with whom he was little acquainted, his plans were not kept so secret as they might otherwise have been, and the faithful old Cæsar thus got information respecting them.

CHAPTER XII

SOME hours passed quietly away at Mr. Jefferson's country-house after all the preparations had been made for the reception of their expected assailants, and yet no enemy appeared.

Higson and the other leaders had some difficulty in bringing up their forces to the attack. They had discovered that the house had been fortified, and they were well aware that a victory could not be obtained without a considerable loss to themselves. Higson had been on shore for some weeks before these preparations were made. Sometimes his mind misgave him, especially when he saw that the British troops in the garrison were thoroughly disciplined, and always on the alert, and that even a regiment of black troops, whom it was hoped might be gained over, refused to desert their colours. The conspirators had then, not without a considerable risk, to send to the French and other enemies of England to obtain their assistance. This was readily enough promised, but they were told that they must themselves commence the rebellion, and that then ample assistance would be forthcoming. At length Higson and his associates gained courage, and they hoped by an attack on Mr. Jefferson's house, and by the capture of so many persons of consequence, to obtain an influence over the rest of the people of the island which would at once give them the upper hand.

Several hours of the night had passed away; Lady Sophy and Lady Nora, with the rest of the ladies, were advised to lie down, it being hoped, that perhaps after all, an attack might not be made. Scouts were, however, sent out to watch for the approaching enemy. At length two of them came hurrying back, announcing that they heard the approach of feet up from the sea. This was the most assailable side of the house. The stream, which has been spoken of with its precipitous banks, circled round two sides, while a high cliff, the summit of which was inaccessible, formed another side of the grounds. In front also, the ground sloped rapidly down, so that unless by steps, which had been strongly barricaded, no one could approach up from the sea, even on that side, without considerable difficulty. The Earl and his friends at length observed through certain look-out places, which had been formed on the roof of the upper story, that a large body of men were scaling the hill in a somewhat irregular manner. At first they came on in silence, but on a warm fire being opened upon them, they gave vent to loud shouts and shrieks, and rushed as rapidly up the hill as the nature of the ground would allow them. At the same time a number of persons in the rear lighted torches, which they bore in their hands, and shook them wildly about, as if to terrify those they came to attack. Perhaps also, they believed that by this means they would distract the attention of the besieged, and prevent them taking a steady aim at those in the front. The sight of the torches raised in Mr. Jefferson's mind an apprehension which he had not before entertained. He knew too well the cumbustible nature of his dwelling and that if it entered the minds of the rebels, they might without difficulty set the house on fire.

"If they do," he thought, "we must retreat by the back of the house and defend ourselves under the cliffs. We may still perhaps be able to hold our own against these fellows until assistance comes, but the poor ladies, I tremble for them."

He did not, however, express these apprehensions to the Earl, but, like a brave man, did his best to encourage those around him. As the enemy approached, they opened a fire at the doors and windows of the house, but as these had been well barricaded, the bullets fell harmlessly against them. A considerable number of the rebels were soon struck down, either killed or wounded. Those in the house did not fire until the enemy approached near. The greater number of them were good marksmen. All knew, likewise, that they fought for their lives, and for the lives of those most dear to them. At length Barry proposed sallying out and endeavouring to put the enemy to flight.

"The time may come for that by and by," said Mr. Jefferson. "In the meantime let us be content to hold our own till assistance can arrive from the town, or till the rebels have discovered that they are incapable of overcoming us."

The men who were waving the torches had hitherto not ventured near the house, but had contented themselves with springing here and there and attempting to dazzle the eyes of the besieged party. Higson, who had himself hitherto kept under shelter, now began to fear that his allies would give way, and the attack would altogether fail. He knew the nature of buildings in the West Indies; and finding that the little garrison were not likely to be overcome by the present mode of attack, he determined to set fire to the house, and then to seize those who were likely to prove most valuable to him, as they were escaping from the burning building. He immediately issued an order to the men with torches to rush forward, at the same time directing others to collect all the dry brushwood they could find, and to pile it up in the verandah. Those, however, who first advanced were received with so hot a fire that several were killed or wounded, and the rest sought safety in flight. Again and again Higson urged them to renew the attempt, and finding this did not avail, he ordered the main body to retreat, greatly to the relief of the garrison. The whole body of their enemies were seen descending the hill, and they began to congratulate themselves that they had gained an easy victory. No one had been killed within the house, although several had been struck by bullets which had found their way through the loopholes or the too thinly planked windows.

The Earl and his friends were not left long in doubt about the intentions of the rebels. In a short time they were seen rushing up the hill again, numbers bearing bundles of reeds and other combustible substances, and others flaming torches in their hands. In spite of the hot fire with which they were received, they dashed forward and threw the bundles into the verandah. Several fell in the attempt, but the great mass persevered and the men with the torches now advancing, cast them amidst the heaps of brushwood. In a few seconds the whole was in a blaze. The woodwork of the building soon caught fire, and it became evident to the besieged that the house would not long be tenable. Still, as long as any could remain on the front side, they continued to fire at the rebels.

Mr. Jefferson now called a Council of War, and explained to his friends the plan he proposed for effecting their escape. The Earl agreed that the undertaking was feasible, though they might be exposed to far greater peril than they had hitherto been; still it was the only one, since the house could no longer be held, for when once the flames had gained entire possession of it, the negroes and Caribs would probably make a dash forward through the fire and put all they could meet with to death. Hitherto none of the rebels had ventured to go round to the rear of the house. Indeed, when any had tried to pass by either of the sides, they had met with so warm a fire that even the boldest had not dared to proceed, while many had been struck down in the attempt.

"We must place the ladies in our centre and retreat to the cliff," said Mr. Jefferson.

Lord Fitz Barry and three or four of the men agreed suddenly to burst open the door, and then

lead the way in the direction Mr. Jefferson had in-
dicated. The plan was adopted, while some of the
men continued to fire down upon their assailants.

The ladies were carried safely out, surrounded by
an armed party, to the rear of the house. Not until
they had been placed in comparative safety did the
rest of the men withdraw from their now almost
untenable position. At length the whole front of
the house was in flames. The fire soon caught the
rest of the building, and scarcely had the last de-
fender left it, than the combustible roof fell in with
a loud crash. The negroes shouted and shrieked
with glee when they saw this, and rushed forward as had been anticipated, in the hopes of
gaining an easy victory over their now defenceless
opponents.

Many of them were severely burnt, as they dashed
forward into the building, and were glad again
quickly to retreat. Not till the whole edifice was
one blazing heap, did they discover that the inmates
had escaped them. By the light of the flames which
continued burning brightly, the negroes perceived
the Lieutenant Governor and the planters with their
families posted at the side of the cliff.

For some time, warned by the treatment they had
received, they hesitated to advance, but at length
Higson, animated by the success which had already

attended his efforts, rushed forward, calling to his men to follow him, and made a dash towards the Earl. He thought that if he could once get him into his power, the victory would be gained. The negroes were perfectly ready to follow when others led, and thus a band of shouting, shrieking wretches, advanced close to where the European party had taken shelter. Already many had begun to climb the heights, and a stout black ruffian had actually got so close, that he was able to lay his hand upon the Earl's shoulder. Higson shouted to the man to drag forward the Governor, in order to make him prisoner. At that moment Fitz Barry, seeing the danger that his father was in, sprang forward to his rescue, and with a blow of his cutlass, compelled the man to let go his hold. In the meantime, however, Higson, with the runaway seamen, whom he had persuaded to follow him, made a dash at that part of the terrace where the ladies were collected. The dawn had now broken, so that they were soon found without the light from the burning house. Lady Nora, seeing the approach of the ruffians, cried to her brother for help. He, however, found himself surrounded by a number of blacks, who pressed him so hard that he was unable to reach her. In the meantime the planters continued to fire down upon their assailants, the great body of whom were kept at bay. Higson at length turned, and ordered more of his followers to come to his assistance. He had already seized Lady Nora, well satisfied that should he fail to capture the Earl, she, at all events would prove a valuable prize. Two other ladies were also carried off, and in vain did their defenders attempt by a bold dash to rescue them. Higson, elated at his success, and at the same time fearful lest the bullets which were flying about might strike any of his captives, and probably glad himself to avoid them, made a wide circuit to gain the sea-shore.

He was already separated from the main body of the insurgents, when suddenly he was startled with a loud shout close to him, and before he could turn round to defend himself, he was attacked by a body of seamen, led on by a lieutenant. The increasing light revealed to him several of his late shipmates, and the new lieutenant, Mr. Denham. Surprised by the attack, for the boat's crew had sprung upon them from behind a thicket, Higson and his companions at once let go their captives. A blow from the cutlass of one of the men brought him to the ground, while the rest of his party—more than one half were either killed or wounded—sought safety in flight. They were not far from the sea-shore. "You must allow me, Lady Nora, to place you with the other ladies on board the boat," said Denham. "You will there be in safety, and the crew will row off to a short distance, while I, with the rest of my men, go to the rescue of your father, and the remainder of the party." To these plans Lady Nora willingly agreed, and in a few minutes she found herself with her friends on board a man-of-war's boat, which, with four men, pulled off out of gun-shot from the shore. Anxiously she watched what was taking place, as far as she could see. Still the firing continued, and Lieutenant Denham and his party hurrying again up the hill, she soon lost sight of them amongst the woods. Deep was her anxiety for her father and brother, and Lady Sophy, who remained with the planters and their friends, while she could not help feeling anxious for the risk to which the young lieutenant and his small party of men were exposed, in the presence of so large a body of rebels.

The outhouses and other buildings on the estate had now caught fire, and their flames showed the insurgents still clustering round the side of the hill, though the continued discharge of musketry in the far distance made her hope that the Earl and his party were still defending themselves. Now the fire of the English party seemed to slacken; now more dark forms were seen climbing up the hill. Then again, the defenders of the height increased their fire, and even at that distance she fancied she could hear the shouts of the combatants. At length her attention was drawn off the scene, by hearing one of the crew exclaim, "Here comes the frigate," and she saw rising above a woody point on one side of the bay, the snow-white sails of the *Cynthia*, as close-hauled she stood along the land. The sound of the firing must have reached her. She immediately hauled into the bay. The anchor was dropped, the sails furled, and several boats were seen to come off from her side. In a short time the boats approached, and the men informed the officers in them of the orders they had received from Lieutenant Denham, adding that they had three ladies in their boat. "Take the ladies to the frigate," answered one of the officers; "give way, my lads, there is no time to be lost." The boats dashed on. Nora thanked Heaven for their arrival, hoping by this means those she dearly loved might be saved, as well as those friends, whose hospitality they had been enjoying. The boats quickly reached the beach, and the men, all well armed, dashed forward up the hill, led by their officers. Attacking the enemy fiercely in the flank, the latter, who had apparently not seen their approach were taken by surprise. Those who resisted were cut down, the rest taking to flight along the shore. No one stopped to look behind him or see what had become of his neighbour. The seamen quickly scaled the heights, and reached the spot where the Earl and his party still held their position. Unhappily several had been badly wounded, among whom were two of the ladies, and three or four planters, while others had been killed. Of the insurgents, a very considerable number had been struck down. The wounded now began to utter loud shrieks and groans, to excite the commiseration of their conquerors. At present, however, little could be done for them. Those of the English who had been wounded were at once conveyed on board the frigate, where they could receive medical treatment. Indeed so alarmed had the planters become, that they requested that they and their families might be taken on board with the Earl. The frigate lay at anchor in the bay. As soon as those who had been wounded on the side of the planters had been cared for, the assistant-surgeon with a boat's crew was humanely sent on shore to attend to the unhappy blacks and Caribs who had been hurt. A few had in the meantime crawled off. Others had died, but still a considerable number remained and required attention. Among the dead was found the unhappy Higson. No one knew what could have induced him to join in so mad a scheme, but those who had watched his conduct on board were not surprised at his behaviour.

On the return of the frigate to the chief town, it was found that the garrison had been warned in time. A considerable number of troops had marched unmolested through the country, visiting the places which were said to be most disaffected, and in a few days the rebel forces had completely melted away. A few men who were caught and accused of leading the rebellion suffered the penalty of death, others had managed to make their escape from the island. It was found, however, that they had been instigated to the rebellion by foreign emissaries, and even the captive rebels themselves acknowledged they had few causes of complaint against the English government.

CHAPTER XIII.

THE outbreak being thus speedily quelled, the
Earl was enabled very soon to return in
safety to his country residence. He had there a
severe affliction awaiting him. Owing either to
the over-exertions made by Lord Fitz Barry on
the night of the attack at the planter's house, or
from some other cause, his disease from that time
gained rapid ground. His friend Denham now felt
greatly alarmed at the change which he remarked
in him, and saw too clearly that he was destined
to remain but a short time longer on earth. The
surgeon also, who had known him some years, was
of the same opinion. Captain Falkner felt, though
most reluctantly, that it was his duty to convey
the sad information to his father and sister. The
Earl refused to believe it, but Nora saw, with grief,
the sad change which even a few days had made
in her beloved brother. He could now only sit up
for a short time in an arm-chair.

In consequence of the rebellion the *Cynthia* had

to remain for some time in the harbour, and accordingly Denham was able to obtain leave to remain with his friend. He and Nora, therefore, were constantly by the side of the dying youth. Barry would not for some time believe that his own end was approaching. Often, with tears in her eyes, Nora spoke to him of that happy land to which all those who trust in the Rock of Ages are certainly bound.

"There will be no more sorrow, no more suffering, no more fighting, no more wounds in that land, dear Barry," she said, taking his hand. "Still, life is sweet. I wish you could have remained with us; but we must bow to God's will. They say you have not many more days to remain on earth, Barry; but surely we must feel the parting more severely—we who have to remain in this world exposed to so many dangers, than you should, who have to go to that land of joy and rest."

The young lieutenant shook his head.

"It is hard for me to acknowledge that, dear Nora," he answered. "I care not for the dangers; and there are so many things to enjoy in this life, that I had hoped to remain in it to a good old age. I have everything to make life pleasant, and can you be surprised, then, that I should be unwilling to quit it without a sigh?"

"O! no, no," she answered. "I know that; but still, remember, it is but to enter into a life of eternal joy that you leave this world of trials. Because, let us deceive ourselves as we may, there are many causes which must bring us sorrow and pain. You remember how we grieved when our dear mother was taken from us, and then it was very sad to leave the old castle, and then, too, we have sorrowed on account of our father, that his property has suffered so much, and though we have been very lovingly dealt with by God, yet He has not allowed life to be so delightful to us that we should be willing to remain here for ever."

Denham spoke to his friend in the same strain. Often did his heart swell within him as he had to address the dying youth, and many a time he dashed away from his eyes the fast-falling tears as he thought that in a few days they must part, never again to meet in this world. He had seen several of his shipmates cut down by the sword of the enemy. Young as he was, death was no stranger to him. The saddest loss he had ever yet experienced was that of his brave and gentle friend, with his youth and rank and many noble qualities. Even to the end, which came at last, the Earl could not believe that his son was dying.

It was daytime. The soft breeze came in through

the open window. He sat, as usual, in his chair, with his sweet sister on one side and his friend Denham on the other. His hands were placed in theirs. He felt that he was about to take his departure.

"Kiss me, Nora," he said.

Denham felt him press his hand for an instant; then the fingers relaxed, and he sank back, and they both saw that his spirit had fled.

Nora did not give way to tears; her grief was too deep for that. Denham felt that he could not venture to comfort her; he dared not even trust his voice in words. Happily, Sophy came in, and the attendants were summoned, and Nora was led away to her chamber.

Denham's leave had just then expired. He went to pay his farewell respects to the Earl; but Lord Kilfinnan entreated him to remain.

"I will write to Captain Falkner," he said. "He will not insist upon your returning on board just now. I must have you with me. You are my son's dearest friend. I know that from the way he spoke of you. I cannot let you go. You must stop and comfort a broken-hearted old man. And poor Nora, she will feel his death dreadfully. Well, 'God's will be done;' perhaps, after all, the poor lad would have found that he had but a scant inheritance to support his title."

Denham remained in the house as desired, having obtained leave from Captain Falkner to do so.   He occasionally saw Lady Nora, who spoke to him kindly and gently, as she naturally would do to her late brother's friend.   Lady Sophy was far more cordial in her manner.   He, however, conversed but little with the Earl.   Indeed, it was very evident that Lord Kilfinnan could not trust his voice to speak about his son.   After the funeral Denham once more returned on board.

CHAPTER XIV.

AGAIN the *Cynthia* sailed on a cruise. She had to visit various parts of the West Indies; sometimes cruising off the Leeward, and sometimes off the Windward Islands. Now to convoy a fleet of merchant vessels from one port to another, and occasionally to accompany them part of the way across the Atlantic, till they were clear of the region infested by the enemy's smaller privateers.

Several months were thus occupied in a somewhat tedious manner. Small prizes had been taken; but these did not satisfy the ardent mind of the gallant captain, who appeared to be longing to meet an enemy the size of his own frigate, a more worthy competitor than any of the vessels he had hitherto encountered. At length, Captain Falkner and his young lieutenant were enabled once more to pay a visit to the Earl and his family. Denham was received as kindly as before; and it was very evident the affection existing between Lady Sophy and Captain Falkner had in no way decreased.

During the last day of his stay on shore, however, a degree of melancholy seemed to weigh down his captain at times. Occasionally he talked in his usual lively and animated manner, and spoke hopefully of the future, when, the war being ended, he might with honour sheath his sword and take up his abode on shore.

"At present, however," he remarked, "while my country demands my services I am bound to remain afloat."

The frigate, however, was again ordered to sea, and the lovers parted, hoping ere long to meet again. Captain Falkner was unusually silent during his drive to the port, and when he arrived on board he retired to his cabin, and it was not until the moment the ship had to get under weigh he appeared on deck. He was then as full of life and activity as usual, and issued his orders in that clear ringing voice by which he was so well known. As the frigate under all sail stood out to sea, Denham more than once observed his captain turning his glass towards the governor's house high up on the mountain side. In his mind's eye he probably saw her who had so deservedly won his brave heart, though the distance was in reality too great to have discovered any human being. Denham felt very much inclined to imitate his commander's example;

but though he lifted his telescope, he quickly lowered it again.

"No, no; what folly in me to indulge in so idle a dream," he said to himself, turning away. "I was received as Barry's friend, and treated with kindness accordingly; but I should only deservedly bring down scorn and ridicule on myself if I were ever to aspire to a greater intimacy than that which has hitherto been allowed me."

"Well, Denham, we must not return without an enemy's frigate in tow," observed Captain Falkner, as he was one day walking the deck, with his young lieutenant. "The Frenchmen have several fine vessels out in these seas at present, and we must try and diminish their numbers. Let us but catch sight of one of them, and, unless she has a very fast pair of heels, she shall be our prize before many hours are over."

"No doubt of that, sir," answered Denham, laughing. "We have now as fine a ship's company as were ever collected together, having cleared out the black sheep who were among them, and they are in as good temper as men need be."

"A sail on the lee-bow," shouted the look-out from aloft.

"What is she like?" asked the captain.

"A full-rigged ship, sir," was the answer.

There was a fresh northerly breeze at the time, and the frigate was under easy sail.

"Turn the hands up, Mr. Hansom," observed the captain to the first lieutenant. "Make all sail."

"All hands on deck," shouted the boatswain, piping his whistle at the same time.

The crew speedily made their appearance, and in a few seconds were seen clustering on the yards aloft. The ship was kept away, studding-sails and royals were set; and the frigate, gliding rapidly over the water, stood towards the stranger. The latter, though she must have seen her coming, showed no inclination to avoid her; but, on the contrary, hauled her wind, that they might the sooner meet. Every spy-glass was in requisition on board the *Cynthia*, and most of the officers went aloft, that they might take a better view of the stranger. In a short time she was pronounced to be a frigate of equal size to their own. Some, however, thought her larger. That she might be so, and under an enemy's flag, was the wish of all. It is strange how eager men are to encounter those they consider it lawful to engage with in fight, to wound and slay each other. They think not of the pain and suffering they may inflict, or may themselves undergo. They eagerly seek for the excitement of the strife, the triumph of victory. They seem to forget entirely what far greater triumphs await those who labour on in civil life to advance the interests of humanity, to win the desert from barrenness, to make it smile as a fruitful garden, and the glorious triumph which is reserved for those who struggle on bravely in the service of their Heavenly Lord and Master. Still, we are describing men as they are, not as they should be; and probably on board that frigate there was not a single man who had the slightest doubt that the sentiments which animated his bosom were otherwise than right and noble, and superior to all others.

A shout burst from the mouths of the crew of the *Cynthia* when the French flag was seen to be run up to the peak of the stranger. She was standing on with all plain sail set, and was manœuvring in order to gain the weather-gauge. The *Cynthia's* studding-sails and more lofty canvas having been taken in, she also tacked in order not to let her antagonist gain this advantage. At length they approached sufficiently near each other to allow the bow guns of the *Cynthia* to take effect.

"Mr. Hansom, let us see if we cannot knock away some of her spars," observed the captain.

"Ay, ay, sir," answered Mr. Hansom, going forward and taking the match in his hands.

There was a good deal of sea running at the time, so that the aim, even of the best marksman, was likely to prove uncertain. He waited his opportunity however. As the bows of the frigate rose he applied the match, and some white splinters were seen to fly from the enemy's topmast. A cheer burst from the throats of the crew who saw the success of the experiment. It was looked upon as a good omen for the future. The cheer, however, was repressed by the officers. The men stood at their quarters. The captains of guns with their matches in their hands, most of them stripped to the waist, to allow them the better to work the tackles, and also, should they be wounded, to escape the injury which any piece of clothing was sure to cause, should it be carried into their bodies by the shot. It was a scene which a painter might have delighted to copy, exhibiting the sturdy forms of the seamen, their countenances determined and bold, and utterly devoid of any appearance of fear. Many, indeed, were passing rough and coarse jokes one from the other, and the slightest excuse gave cause to a hearty laugh. It would have been difficult for a stranger to believe, that the men who were before him were entering into a struggle for life and death, or that the combat between the two beautiful frigates now sailing in sight of each other, would probably end in the destruction of one of them. Each sail was well set, every yard perfectly braced, and all the ropes taut and uninjured. Thus they stood on, slowing nearing each other, till at length the Frenchman attempted to haul across the *Cynthia's* bows, for the purpose of delivering a raking fire. This the latter avoided by hauling up.

"Fire," cried the captain, as the broadside of the frigate bore upon that of the enemy. A loud roar of artillery was the response. Several shots seemed to take effect, some in the hull, others in the rigging. The *Cynthia* herself did not escape injury, and two of her crew were seen struggling in their death agonies on the deck. The two frigates now ran on side by side, firing their guns as rapidly as they could be loaded. Again a shout burst from the throats of the English crew, as the Frenchman's fore-topmast was seen to go over the side. It was evident, too, that their shots were taking effect upon the Frenchman's hull, for several were seen to strike him between wind and water, which with the sea then running was very likely in a short time to reduce him into a sinking state. Still the latter worked his guns with as much determination as at first, aided by musketry whenever the ships approached near enough for the bullets to take effect. By this means a considerable number of the crew of the English frigate were struck down, many of whom were killed, while others were carried bleeding below.

The superior strength and activity of the English seamen soon told against that of the enemy, for while the latter were delivering two broadsides the English managed to fire three, their shot, too, being better directed. Still the French ensign flew out at the enemy's peak, and there appeared to be no intention on his part of lowering it. The contest was evidently to be a severe and protracted one. The *Cynthia* had already lost nearly thirty of her crew, and in all probability the Frenchman must have suffered in a far greater degree. At length they drew so close that the muzzles of their guns almost touched, when the enemy, putting down his helm, ran his bows into those of the British ship, the bowsprit coming directly across the foremast. Captain Falkner, calling to Denham and those who were near him at the time, sprang forward and attempted to lash the bowsprit to the mast of his own ship. Denham saw his faithful follower, Ned Davis, by his side. While the captain was in the act of passing a rope round the mast, a bullet from the musket of a marine stationed in the Frenchman's top, struck him on the breast. He fell back, and Denham had just time to catch him in his arms to save him from falling heavily upon the deck. Davis had at that moment seized the rope which the captain had let go.

DEATH OF CAPTAIN FALKNER.

"Secure the bowsprit," cried the captain; "do not let the enemy sheer off. Now place me on the deck; I fear that I am mortally wounded, but do not let the people know it. In a few minutes the Frenchman's frigate will be ours. See, they are attempting to board, but drive them back and they will not long keep their flag flying. On! on! do not heed me."

Denham, calling to some of the crew, ordered them to take the captain below, while he flew to obey his dying orders.

"Boarders, repel boarders," he shouted, drawing his own sword, and springing towards the point where the Frenchmen were seen clustering in their rigging about to spring on the deck of the *Cynthia*. The latter, already disheartened by the loss of so many of their shipmates, were quickly driven back, while the *Cynthia's* guns continued pouring broadside after broadside into the hull of their ship.

"See, see, down goes the French flag," cried the English crew, and little knowing the loss they had sustained, they once more gave forth that hearty British cheer which has so often sounded in the moment of victory. The dying captain heard it as Denham reached his side.

"Tell her my last thoughts were about her," he murmured as the lieutenant took his hand, and sinking back, his eyes were in another moment closed by the hand of death.

The two ships had parted in consequence of the heavy sea which had now got up. For the same reason the task of transferring the crew of the prize to the victor was one of considerable difficulty. The first lieutenant, now in command of the *Cynthia*, hailed the enemy to send a boat on board; but his reply was that he had none which would swim, all having been injured in the engagement. Fortunately most of the *Cynthia's* boats were in a better condition, and Denham, taking the command, at once proceeded on board the prize. He found, though the frigate was French, that a Dutch officer commanded her, who seemed much down-hearted at the loss of his ship.

The young lieutenant had already been in several engagements, but never had he seen a deck present a more sad spectacle than that of the Frenchman. In all directions lay the bodies of the slain, and several wounded men who had not yet been conveyed below. They were all of them too much injured to be removed to the *Cynthia*, and they were therefore carried below. The prisoners were at once ordered to get up their bags, and to enter the boats, which immediately conveyed them on board their captor.

Some time was occupied, however, in this work, as the heavy sea which now ran prevented them from making a rapid passage. The Dutch officer commanding the ship, had given up his sword to Lieut. Denham, who remained on board, ready to take charge of the prize. He himself had not had time to go below, to observe the damages that the prize had sustained, but from the report made to him by the late commander, he was under the apprehension that they were very severe. Indeed, from the peculiar way the ship rolled, he dreaded that she had taken in a large amount of water. He accordingly requested the Dutchman, who spoke English very well, to send his carpenter below, to make a report of her condition. The man in a short time returned on deck with a pale face, declaring he did not believe she would float for many hours longer. By this time the wind had increased so much, and so heavy a sea was running, that it was a matter of danger to pass between the two ships, which were at some distance from each other. The boats, with the last cargo of the prisoners, had left her, and were close alongside of the *Cynthia.* Denham therefore ordered his own crew to make every effort to stop the leaks, but they soon found, from the amount of water which was pouring in, that this would be difficult, if not impossible.

"Well," he remarked to the Dutchman, after every effort had been made to put a stop to the entrance of the water, "as soon as the boats return, we must, I fear, abandon the ship. You have defended her nobly, and perhaps have less cause to regret this occurrence than we have, who hoped to carry her into port in triumph." ·

" You of course will return to your own ship as you please," answered the Dutch officer; "but for my part I cannot desert my poor wounded fellows below, and unless there is time to remove them, should the ship sink beneath my feet, I must go down with her."

CHAPTER XV.

I N vain Denham urged the brave Dutchman to
save his own life, and promised to use his best
exertions in removing those who were least hurt
among the wounded men. He was looking anxiously for the return of the boats. One, however,
only was seen to put off from the side of the frigate
with the remainder of the prize crew, Mr. Hansom
deeming it imprudent to allow more than necessary to make the passage. It was not without considerable difficulty that this boat reached the side
of the prize. Again Denham urged the captain to
quit her, but he refused on the same plea as before.
Indeed, it was very evident the boat herself would
only carry in one trip the prize crew. Denham had
ordered all the men to go into the boat, and at
length finding that the Dutchman persisted in remaining on board, he could not bring himself to
desert the brave fellow.

"Well," he said, "I will remain too, and assist
the men on board to keep the ship afloat, for I feel

I have no business to detain my own people with so great a risk."

"If you remain, Mr. Denham, so will I," exclaimed Ned Davis, who had followed his friend. "It may be, if we keep the pumps going, that the ship will float until there is time to get more boats alongside."

Before he allowed the boat to shove off Denham wrote a short note to Mr. Hansom, begging him, unless the sea continued to increase, to send boats to carry off the wounded people; "but," he concluded his note, "should it do so, run no risk of losing any lives—leave us to the care of God."

The boat shoved off, and the sinking frigate was left to struggle alone amidst the fast-rising sea.

The French crew, encouraged by the example of their gallant captain, exerted themselves to the utmost to stop the leak, while those not thus occupied stood manfully at the pumps. By this means the sorely battered frigate continued to keep afloat, but each time the well was sounded it was found that the water had gained somewhat upon her, in spite of all the efforts made to free her of water.

Ned Davis was a host in himself, flying here and there, aiding in stopping shot-holes, and then returning to take his spell at the pumps.

The young lieutenant anxiously looked out for

any signs of change in the weather, but that continued as bad as ever, till it became too evident that the frigate could not much longer be made to swim.

Denham thought of suggesting that the wounded men should be brought on deck to give them a better chance of escaping; but the doctor said they would thus to a certainty perish, and that if the ship went down it would be more merciful to them not to allow them to see the approach of their certain destruction.

The ensign was hoisted upside down, as a sign that the ship was in great distress, and guns were fired to draw the attention of the *Cynthia* to her. Denham anxiously watched the progress of his frigate, feeling sure that from the mode in which the prize laboured in the sea she was not likely to float much longer. In a short time the *Cynthia* bore down upon her, but already the sea ran so high that it was evidently a risk to send a boat; and it would have been almost impossible to lower wounded people into her. Again Denham urged the brave Dutchman, should a boat be sent, to accompany him on board the frigate.

"No," he answered; "I have made up my mind to remain by these people, and nothing shall induce me to desert them."

After some time a boat was seen approaching
14

from the *Cynthia*. Denham now feeling it was his duty to save his own life as well as that of his people, ordered them to take the opportunity as she drew near of leaping into her. A few of the French crew, who were not wounded, followed their example. While Denham remained Davis refused to go into the boat. At length it was evident that at any moment the prize might sink.

"Now," he exclaimed to Davis, "leap into her, and I will follow." He shook the Dutchman warmly by the hand. "You are a brave man, my friend," he said; "and though I would stay by you if I could assist in saving your life, my duty to my men and to myself compels me to leave you."

"Farewell," answered the Dutchman, seemingly unmoved.

"No time to lose, sir," shouted Davis from the boat.

Denham sprang from the side of the vessel; and scarcely had he reached the boat, and taken his seat in the stern-sheets, when the bow of the prize lifted high up above the sea, and then down she sank, lower and lower, till the water washed over her deck, and finally closed again above her masthead.

The frigate's boat had barely time to pull away clear of the vortex. Several people were seen struggling in the waves; among them Denham observed the brave captain, and, though not without great risk, he ordered the boat to pull back, to endeavour to get him on board. Once, as they neared the spot, he disappeared, and Denham feared he was lost for ever. He again, however, rose, when Ned Davis, leaning over the bows, caught hold of his jacket and succeeded in hauling him on board. He was the only person among the prisoners who was saved, for before the boat could reach the others, all disappeared beneath the waves. Happily the boat had no great distance to go, for it was only by great exertions and careful management that she was kept afloat. The whole of the wounded and many others of the French crew perished.

The loss of their prize was a great disappointment to the officers and ship's company of the *Cynthia*, as they had only the bare victory to boast of, without being able to show the prize when they returned into port; but far more did they mourn the death of their brave captain. No one felt it more than Denham. To him he had been a warm and sincere friend, besides which he knew the agony and grief it would cause to one who was expecting his return. He dreaded having personally to communicate what had occurred, and he was greatly relieved by finding that the frigate was to put into Port Royal, Jamaica, to refit after the action.

Mr. Hansom did not forget to mention him in his despatches, as having greatly contributed to gain the victory, by his courage in assisting to lash the enemy's bowsprit to the *Cynthia's* foremast.

"Depend upon it, Denham," observed Mr. Hansom, "this will be marked in your favour at the Admiralty; and when you have served your time as lieutenant, you will obtain a commander's rank. I wouldn't say this to others,—but I have a notion that you have a friend at court, and a word from the Earl, with so good an excuse, will be sure to gain whatever he asks for you."

On reaching Port Royal Denham felt it was his duty to write to the Earl, giving an account of the events that had occurred; but he did not allude even to anything he himself had done, nor did he ask for the Earl's interest for himself at the Admiralty.

Some few months after this Lord Kilfinnan gave up his appointment, and returned with his family to his native land.

CHAPTER XVI.

IN a turret chamber in Kilfinnan Castle sat two
young ladies. It was apparently their private
boudoir. It had been elegantly furnished, but the
drapery had somewhat faded, and the air of fresh-
ness it had once possessed had long since departed.
The window out of which the ladies were gazing
looked forth over the wide Atlantic, and the eldest
was dressed in deep mourning, apparently her usual
costume, while the air of sadness in her countenance seemed to be habitual. The younger one was
full of life and animation, though occasionally, as
she looked up at her friend, she, too, became sad.

"That is a strange story, Sophy, you were reading just now from the newspaper," said the youngest,—"I mean about Lord Eden; I cannot understand how a man of his rank and position should
condescend to marry a girl of low degree, however
virtuous or excellent she might be. These *més-
alliances* can never answer. Too soon the one of
more refined habits and ideas discovers a degree

of coarseness and vulgarity in the other, which must ultimately cause separation. No; my only notion of a happy union is, that where people are of the same rank and education, and all their sympathies are in unison—"

"You know so little of life, dear Nora, that I do not think you are capable of judging," answered her cousin Sophy; "I do not say, however, that in the main you are not right, but there may be exceptions, in which true happiness may be found. I do not say Lord Eden is right in marrying this girl. At the same time, she may have more natural refinement than could be expected. I have heard of such instances."

"I, on the contrary, Sophy, remember hearing my father speak of a very different case, in which a country girl was taken out of her sphere, and educated, and, I think, became the wife of one of our ministers. As long as she was at rest, she appeared very elegant, but if she got at all excited, or, as was sometimes the case, lost her temper, she then exhibited her real condition; and if, as I consider, it is very bad for a man to marry a person of inferior rank, surely it is much worse for a lady to marry one who is her inferior."

Sophy smiled sadly.

"No; I shall hold to my own opinion," said

Nora, "and I do not think that anybody would induce me to marry a person, however elegant and refined he might appear, unless I knew he was of gentle blood."

The conversation of the young ladies was interrupted by Sophy exclaiming,—

"Bring the glass, Nora; I see a vessel standing in for the bay. Her canvas looks very white and shining. I believe she is a man-of-war."

The telescope, which stood on a stand, had been, for some purpose, removed from the window, and it was now brought to its usual place by Nora. They both looked through it, one after the other.

"Yes, there can be no doubt of the matter," said Nora; "her square yards, her tall masts and white canvas show at once what she is. She does not appear to me to be a frigate. I think she is a smaller vessel—a corvette,—and very beautiful vessels they are."

While this conversation was going forward, the ship rapidly approached the shore, under a wide spread of canvas. They had soon an opportunity of ascertaining her character. At length she stood into the bay, and, furling her sails, came to an anchor. The wind was at that time sufficiently from the north to enable her to obtain perfect shelter, and she floated calmly on the smooth waters. It was still early in the day. They watched for a short time, but no boat could put off to approach the castle, though they fancied they saw one standing in for another part of the bay.

At that time Ireland was suffering, as she had long been, from her usual chronic disorder—discontent. Disturbances had occurred here and there in the west and south among the Riband Men, or White Boys, or United Irishmen, by which names the rebels were at different times and places known. The Government, therefore, had considered it necessary to send vessels of war to cruise up and down the coast, that their blue jackets and marines might render such assistance as might be required. This was so generally the case at present, that the arrival of the corvette did not cause any unusual sensation among the inhabitants of the coast who lived near enough the sea to observe her. Several men-of-war had in the same way entered the bay of late, and, after remaining a few days, had taken their departure. The young ladies had arranged that, later in the day, they would take a ride over the downs, and, after calling on Miss O'Reilly, at the vicarage, look in upon some of the poor people whom they were in the habit of visiting.

Meantime, we must go to the other end of the bay, where an old man might be seen descending the narrow gorge which led down to the small cove where the Widow O'Neil resided. It was Father O'Rourke. He proceeded on in a somewhat meditative mood, until he reached the cottage. He opened the door, and found the widow sitting on the usual stool, employed in mending her nets.

" And what brings you here, Father O'Rourke ?" she said, looking up at him with a glance which showed that he was not a favourite of hers.

" Widow, I have come to speak about a matter of importance," he answered. "I hear, in spite of all my warnings, and all the instruction I have given you, by which you would be sure to find your way to heaven, that you still go to that heretic minister, Mr. Jamieson, as you used to do when I before warned you. Now, I tell you, widow, if you love your soul, you must go there no more. I am not going to be warning you for ever. Do you hear my words ? Do you intend to obey them ?"

"Father O'Rourke," said the widow, looking calmly at him, "I have a great respect for your office, and for the holy religion of which you are a priest; there is nothing I have ever said against that. I am a good Catholic, as I have always been, and you shall not be the person to throw a stone at me; but if I go to the vicarage, I go to hear the gentle words of that poor blind lady, and the minister never speaks anything to me but what is faithful and true. He is a good man, Father O'Rourke, and I wish I was as sure of going to heaven as he is: that is what I have got to tell you."

"Oh, Widow O'Neil, those are evil words you are speaking!" exclaimed the priest; "you are just disobeying the holy mother Church; you are just doing what will bring you down the road to destruction, and I tell you, I believe it was your obstinacy, and your love for those heretics, that was the cause of the loss of your son. He is gone, and I hope he is gone to glory, for it is not for the want of me saying masses for his soul, if he has not; for sure I am, that, if he had remained here, and listened longer to the instruction of that false heretic, he would have gone the way you are so anxious to go, Widow O'Neil."

The widow now stood up, throwing from her the nets, which had hitherto been on her knees. She stepped back a pace or two, and stretched out her hands.

"Father O'Rourke," she exclaimed, "it is not the truth you are speaking to me! My boy never learned anything but what was good when he went to the vicarage: and more than that, though you say he has gone from this world, there is something deep down in my heart which tells me he is still alive. If he were dead, my heart would feel very different to what it does now. I tell you, Father O'Rourke, I believe my son is alive, and will come back some day to see me. I know he will. Do you think I doubt his love? Do I doubt my love for him? No. Father O'Rourke, you are a childless man yourself, and you do not know what the love of a mother is for her child, and I do not think you know what the love of a child is for its mother—a fond, loving mother, as I have been,—not such a child as mine. The day will come when Dermot will stand here, as you are standing here; but he will not be blaming his old mother as you are blaming her. He will come to speak words of comfort and consolation into my ear. Instead of that, Father O'Rourke, you have brought nothing but cursing. You tell me I am in the downward road to destruction. Is that the way you should speak to a lone widow, because she loves her son, and likes those to speak who knew him, and who would talk about him to her and praise him, and who tell her what a noble, clever youth he was?"

"Widow O'Neil!" exclaimed Father O'Rourke, an angry frown gathering on his brow, "year after year I have spoken to you as I am now speaking. I have warned you before, I have warned your boy Dermot. I tell you, he would not take the warning, and he would have suffered the consequences of his disobedience, but I do care for your soul, and it is on account of that soul that I want you to put faith in the holy mother Church. If you do, all will be right, but if you go and listen to the words of that Protestant minister, all will be wrong, and you, Widow O'Neil, will have to go and live for ever with the accursed; ay, for ever and ever in fire and torment." With such force and energy did the priest speak, and so fierce did he look, that for the moment he made the poor old woman tremble and turn pale with fear. She quickly, however, recovered herself.

"You may go, Father O'Rourke," she exclaimed. "Once I was your slave, but I am your slave no longer. I am a poor ignorant woman, but I have had the truth told me, and that truth has made me free of you; say what you will, I do not fear you."

The priest on hearing these words positively stamped on the ground, and gnashed his teeth with anger. He was not one of the polished fathers of the Church, who have been taught from their youth to conceal their feelings. He was certainly not a trained disciple of Ignatius Loyola. Again and again he stamped, and then uttering a fearful anathema on the occupant of the hut, he turned round, and slamming the door, left her as he had often before done, and hastened upwards towards the cliffs. While this scene was enacting below, a young naval officer, who had landed from a boat which had come from the corvette, lately brought up in the bay, had climbed to the summit of the downs, and was taking his way across them towards the gorge, up which the priest was hastening. He had, however, not got very far, when he heard a voice singing a wild and plaintive Irish air. He stopped to listen, and as he did so, a figure, dressed in fantastic fashion, appeared from behind some broken ground in the neighbourhood of the downs. She advanced towards him, and then suddenly stopped, looking eagerly in his face.

"Who are you, stranger—who are you who come to these shores? It is not good for you to be alone here; if you come, come with armed men, with muskets on their shoulders and swords by their sides, for that slight weapon that you carry would avail you nothing against the enemies you are likely to meet here. Go back, I tell you, the way you came. I may seem silly and mad, and mad and silly I am, but I can sing; few can sing like me. Now listen, stranger, listen to my song." She burst forth again in the same wild strains which at first attracted the young officer's attention.

"But what reason could you give me why I should

follow your advice ? I like your song, however; can you not sing me another ?"

"Yes," she answered, "Mad Kathleen has many a song in her head, but it does not always come when called for, it is only as the fit seizes her that she can bring it forth. Never mind listening to my song, however, but follow my advice. There is your boat even now out in the bay; go, make a signal to it to come back to you, or evil will befall you."

"I can scarcely suppose that, provided I do not leave the shore," answered the officer. "I thank you, however, for your advice, but I do not purpose wandering far from where I now am."

"Even here where you stand you are not safe; but I have warned you once, and I cannot warn you more," exclaimed the mad woman, as with wild gestures she retreated back to the spot from which she appeared to have come. The young officer watched her till she disappeared. A shade of melancholy came over his countenance.

"I might have asked her about some of the people hereabouts," he said to himself. "Her warning perhaps is not to be despised; I will sit down here, and wait till the boat returns."

The officer was approaching the edge of the cliff when Father O'Rourke reached the downs; seeing the stranger, he advanced towards him. The temper of the priest had not calmed down, so it seemed, since his encounter with the poor widow. As he approached the young officer, he looked at him earnestly.

"What brings you here?" he exclaimed. "What business have armed men to come upon our coasts, let me ask you?"

"Really, sir," said the officer, drawing himself up, "I bear his Majesty's commission as commander of yonder sloop of war, and in the performance of my duty, I have landed on the shores of this bay; but I do not understand why I should be thus roughly spoken to by one especially, who, judging from his appearance, is a Catholic priest."

"You judge rightly, young man," answered Father O'Rourke, "but I am not to be deceived by appearances, and though you may call yourself what you will, I suspect you to be either the commander of a privateer, if not rather of a vile buccanier. We have had visits before now from such gentry, and I should advise you to leave our shores without delay."

"I cannot understand your meaning," exclaimed the officer; "I repeat, I came here in the performance of my duty, and I little expected to be treated thus by the first stranger I might meet."

The priest seemed to think that he had proceeded

too far; whatever might have been his motive in thus insulting one whom he must have known was a naval officer, or for some reason, he thought fit suddenly to change his tactics.

"Pardon me, sir," he said in a soothing voice, which he well knew how to assume, "I see that I was mistaken in my first supposition, and to prove my sincerity, I shall be happy if I can render to you any service in my power."

"I willingly accept your apologies," answered the officer, regarding the priest intently, as if to ascertain whether he was to be trusted. "On my way along the shore, I intend visiting some of the little coves I see to the northward of these downs, and now, sir, perhaps you can inform me whether I am likely to find any people residing among them?"

"But few, if any," answered the priest, "they are nearly all dead or gone away who once lived there; the curse of your country has been upon them. The aged and the young, the married and the single, the widow and her children, have all been swept away."

"Yes, I have heard that great changes have taken place in this neighbourhood of late years," answered the young officer, a shade of melancholy crossing his countenance. "And now, sir, in spite of the somewhat rough way in which you first addressed me, I wish you good morning, and thank you for your information."

Father O'Rourke had, all the time he was speaking, been examining the countenance of the young officer.

"Ah, to be sure, I was somewhat irritated by a trifle just before I met you, but your politeness has conquered me," he answered blandly, "and I beg you, should you come near my humble abode, to believe that I shall be happy to receive you. We poor, oppressed Catholics have little to offer our guests, but to such as I possess you will be welcome. Our business is to look after the souls of our parishioners. If we can but show them the right way to heaven we should be content."

The young officer seemed somewhat inclined to smile at these remarks of the priest.

"I will not fail to avail myself of your invitation," he answered, "but at present I do not intend to extend my walk along the sea-shore."

"Well then, sir, as you have wished me good morning, I must wish you the same, and a pleasant walk to you, only let me advise you to be cautious where you go; it isn't just the safest part of the country for a king's officer to be found wandering in by himself. However, sir, I have given you a friendly warning, and now again farewell."

15

The priest, somewhat to the surprise of the officer, considering the father's previous greeting, put out his hand, which he was too courteous not to take, then quickly turning round, Father O'Rourke proceeded up the gorge into the country.

Father O'Rourke was not accustomed to explain to others the object of his proceedings. He had good reasons in his own estimation for everything that he did. They were possibly conscientious, but then his conscience might have been a very erring guide, and led him far wrong, as is the case with many other people in the world.

"It cannot be helped," said the priest to himself, alluding to something which was passing in his own mind, "but no harm may come of it to me after all. The boys were to meet at O'Keef's last night, and there will be plenty of them still about there; they will be glad enough of the chance of getting hold of a king's officer, and if he shows fight and some one gives him a knock on the head or sends a pistol-bullet through him, it will settle the business. He is certain to be down in the cove, and if the boys are quick they will catch him there. I am pretty sure that I am not mistaken, but at all events he will be a valuable prize if he can be got hold of any way."

Such thoughts occupied the mind of the priest as turning off from the beaten path he took his way across a mountainous region which still remained in all its primitive wildness. After proceeding for some distance at a speed which was surprising considering his age, he reached some rude turf-covered huts, scarcely discernible from the rocks and grass amid which they stood. The priest gave a peculiar call, which soon brought out a number of shaggy-looking heads and eager faces with grey frieze-coats beneath them. Father O'Rourke did not take long to explain the object of his visit, which was quickly comprehended, nor did he wrongly estimate the inclinations of his hearers, who gleefully undertook to carry out the plan he proposed to them. All things being arranged to his satisfaction he returned to his own abode, saying to himself, "I warned him of danger, so that if he is attacked and escapes he cannot accuse me of having anything to do in the matter."

The officer was about to prosecute his intention of descending into the cove, when he heard merry voices near him. The speakers seemed to be climbing up the cliffs, and they soon made their appearance on its summit. Touching their caps as they neared the officer,—

"The boat has come for you, sir," said one of them.

"Very well," was the answer. "Go down and amuse yourselves on the beach for a short time and I will join you. I am not ready to go off just yet."

The young midshipmen receiving these orders managed to get down the cliffs in a way few but midshipmen could have done without breaking their necks.

"I wonder what our captain's about," said one of them. "I should have thought that he would have gone to the Castle. Lord Kilfinnan lives there, you know; and I remember hearing how constantly he used to be at his house out in the West Indies. Did you ever see Lady Nora?"

"No," answered the other; "I do not remember having heard her spoken of."

"Oh she is the Earl's daughter, and a very beautiful girl she is, too," observed the first speaker. "There is Lady Sophy Danvers, her cousin, too, who lives with her. She was engaged for a long time to that Captain Falkner, you know, who commanded the *Cynthia;* but, I suppose her relations did not like her to marry him because he wasn't a lord, and intended her for a duke or a marquis perhaps."

"I do not see why they should have done that," answered the other midshipman. "In my opinion, a naval officer is equal to any lord in the land; at all events, a post-captain is. If I were a post-captain, I know I should not hesitate to pay my respects to any earl's daughter. Why, just think, to have a fine frigate and three or four hundred men under one's orders, and, by-and-by, a line-of-battle ship, and then a post-captain becomes an admiral, remember; and many admirals have been made lords themselves. Why, there is Lord Nelson; he was only a midshipman to begin with; and Lord Collingwood, and Lord St. Vincent, and Lord Howe, and many others; they were all midshipmen, just as you and I are. Now, just look at our captain for instance; if any one deserves to be made a lord he does. What a gallant fellow he is! Why, if it had not been for him, they say, the *Cynthia* would have been taken. It was he assisted in lashing the enemy's bowsprit to the frigate's foremast, and then repelling the boarders who were swarming on board; and then, there are no end of things he did in the West Indies, and in other parts of the world. He has been in half-a-dozen cutting-out expeditions, and, since he has been a commander, has taken several prizes. Did you ever hear how, when the French frigate was sinking, he refused to leave her, and stayed on board to assist the captain in keeping her afloat at the risk of his own life. Now, that is the sort of thing to be proud of. I often think more of a man who has done those generous actions than one who has gained a hard-fought battle. However, what do you say to having a race along the sands? Here, we will get most of the fellows on shore, and I am ready to give a prize to the best runner."

"I will give my pocket-knife," said the midshipman; "that will be an encouragement to the men. They are good sort of fellows, and I like to afford them amusement. It is little we or they get these days, kept at sea month after month."

As it may be supposed, the young midshipmen were great favourites on board the corvette, and for some time they kept their crew amused as they had proposed. At length they began to wonder that the captain did not appear, and they began to fear that some accident had befallen him. At last they proposed climbing up the cliff again to look for him. They reached the top at last, and looked round the downs on every side; no one was to be seen. Then curiosity led them a short distance inland. Suddenly, a figure which made them start rose up before them.

"Who are you looking for, young sirs?" exclaimed Mad Kathleen. "I know without your telling me. He is gone—gone away, and you must follow to find him; but listen, boys, I have a message for him. Now, don't you fail to give it. Tell him there are enemies watching for him, and that if ever he comes on shore by himself he will be sure to be set upon, and all his strength and courage will avail him nothing. He is a brave man, your captain, and I wish him well."

"Why, how do you know anything about him?" asked one of the midshipmen. "I did not know he had ever been here before."

"Mad Kathleen knows more things than you wot of," answered the mad woman, with a loud laugh, whirling her hands as she spoke. "Now, go to the Castle as I bid you, and give him my message. He would run more risk by neglecting my warning than if he were to fight a dozen battles for his king and country."

Though the midshipmen were little inclined to put much belief in the message of the mad creature, they promised to deliver it as soon as they met their captain. After consulting together, they agreed that their proper course was to row along the bay towards the castle, in the hopes that he might have gone there.

CHAPTER XVII.

AS the commander of the corvette was about to
descend the glen, his attention was arrested by
the faint tramp of horses' hoofs passing rapidly over
the downs. He turned his head and at that instant
saw a young lady on horseback, not far from him,
cantering gaily along, while at a short distance behind her was another lady, followed by a groom.
At that moment the figure of the mad woman, which
had a short time before appeared to him, rose suddenly from behind the ground where he had last
seen her. She uttered a wild shriek; the effect was
to make the leading horse start and rear violently.
The animal apparently, was not well broken in.
Again and again it reared, backing down towards
the edge of the cliff. The young officer saw the
lady's danger, and in an instant sprang towards her.
She uttered a shriek as she discovered how fearfully
near the edge of the cliff her horse had carried her.
The officer grasped her bridle, but in vain tried to
draw back the frightened animal. It seemed re-

DENHAM SAVES NORA.

solved to throw itself over the precipice. In another moment the lady and her steed would have been carried to destruction.

"Throw yourself from your saddle, and trust to me," exclaimed the young officer imploringly.

She cast herself forward and fell into his arms. Alas! her habit caught in the stirrup. Again the horse reared.

"I will perish with her," exclaimed the young man mentally.

Happily, the skirt tore, and in another moment was disengaged; while the frightened animal, with one bound, leaped over the cliff. So extreme was the danger to which the young lady had been exposed, that scarcely knowing she had escaped it, she fainted. The young officer, with his precious burden, hurried up the downs, when her companion, jumping from her horse, came to his assistance.

"O Nora, Nora," she exclaimed, "do tell me that you are alive! O that we had some water to give her, such a faint as this is dangerous. What can be done?"

The groom observing that there was a stream a few hundred yards on, dashed forward on his horse, and quickly returned with his hat full.

Lady Sophy, loosening Nora's dress round her neck, and holding her head on her knee, sprinkled the water over her face, which was turned in the direction of the wind. By this means she quickly returned to consciousness, and, opening her eyes, they fell on the countenance of the young officer.

"Oh, Captain Denham," she exclaimed, "I owe my life to you. In another moment I should have been dashed to pieces. I thought that I had gone over the precipice. How grateful my dear father will be to you!"

"Then that must be your ship," said Lady Sophy, pointing to the corvette. "You must come with us at once to the castle."

Captain Denham, of course, could only express his very great satisfaction at having been the means of preserving the life of Lady Nora, though he could claim no credit for having done so. Whatever had been his previous intentions, he could do nothing else than accompany the ladies till he had seen them safe at the castle. He made anxious inquiries after the Earl, and found, from the account they gave him, that he was greatly broken in health, not having recovered from the effects of the West Indian climate, or the loss of his son. In many respects the meeting could not fail to be a sad one. The sight of Captain Denham recalled painfully to Lady Sophy the death of her intended husband, while Lady Nora, naturally, could not help thinking of her young brother, who had been Captain Denham's friend.

The distance to the castle was considerable, but Lady Nora declared her inability to mount a horse, even if one had been sent for; nor would she consent to take that of Lady Sophy. Supported, however, by the arm of the captain, she proceeded towards home. They had many things to talk about. Captain Denham had to describe how he had been sent to the coast of Ireland to render assistance to any of the loyal subjects of the king who might require it, whilst the ladies described their passage home, and the feelings with which they had · returned once more to the old castle.

"Things are greatly changed," observed Lady Nora, "we have none of the gay society we used to have here; my father also is too much out of spirits to see company. Occasionally a few neighbours look in upon us; or when any ship comes into the bay we see some of the officers, and Mr. Jamieson and dear Miss O'Reilly come over to pay us a visit; but you, Captain Denham, will always be welcome."

Captain Denham and his fair companions had arrived at the castle some time before the midshipmen with the boat appeared, having been joined in the meantime by the second lieutenant.

The Earl welcomed him warmly, and begged him to take up his residence at the castle; but this invitation he was compelled to decline, as he made it a point of duty never to sleep away from the ship at night.

Lady Nora had sufficiently recovered to appear at dinner, to which Denham's officers, who had come on shore, were also invited. Just before dinner Mr. Jamieson and his blind niece arrived. Lady Nora was delighted to see them, and introduced Captain Denham to them both. The blind lady seemed to take especial interest in him. She plied him with questions, asking him what-part of the world he had visited, in what ship he had served, and in what actions he had been engaged.

The Earl had broken through the usual custom of sitting late at dinner; indeed the gentlemen present seemed in no way disposed to follow it. Soon after the ladies had retired, Mr. Jamieson and Captain Denham led the way to the drawing-room. Captain Denham approached Lady Nora and inquired anxiously if she felt perfectly recovered from the effects of her alarming accident.

"Oh, yes; indeed I am," she answered, glancing up at him with a look which might have made many men vain. "I dare not trust myself to thank you as I ought, or to speak about it. I cannot help thinking of what would have been my fate had you not been there to save me. How often have I crossed those downs without dreaming of danger; and indeed it was very curious how that poor mad woman should have startled my horse. I have met her often before, and she has done much the same sort of thing; but the poor animal was young, and had not been ridden for some days. Sophy and I were on our way to visit some of the poor ·people we are accustomed to call upon, and I was anxious to see an old widow who lives in a little cove under where you saw me; but that can be a matter of no interest to you."

As she spoke she again gazed up in his face. Something strange seemed to flash across her mind. She cast another earnest, inquiring look at him. The colour mounted to his cheek. His eyes fell, then again he looked earnestly at her. Nora's breath came and went rapidly; her bosom heaved.

"What is the matter with Nora?" exclaimed Lady Sophy, springing forward, "she is fainting. Help! help!"

In an instant Lady Sophy was by Nora's side, and just in time to receive her as she fell fainting into her arms. Captain Denham stood for an instant so overwhelmed with some deep emotion, as scarcely to comprehend what had occurred.

The bell was rung, and several attendants rushed in, and Nora was borne fainting from the room.

It was still daylight, but just at this moment dark clouds began to collect in the sky, casting a gloom over the landscape. The lieutenant of the corvette had gone to the window looking out over the ocean. He hurriedly came back, and while his commander was standing still bewildered it seemed by what had occurred, he came up to him, and said,—" Sir, there is a change in the weather. The wind has increased considerably, and the bay in a short time will be no place for us." This address aroused Captain Denham.

"You are right, Matson," he answered, looking out at the window for an instant, "I will go on board immediately. We must bid farewell to the Earl and be off. There is not a moment to lose, and I hope Evans will get the ship under weigh without waiting for me."

Just as he was quitting the room Lady Sophy re-entered it, and assured him that Lady Nora had quickly recovered, though still unnerved by the danger she had gone through. "I trust that she will have perfectly recovered by to-morrow," she added. "And, believe me, Captain Denham, you will always be a welcome guest at the castle."

She spoke earnestly, her looks giving expression to her words.

"She is a dear, high-minded girl, and, believe me, I prize her, and will watch over her as a sister, or I should say rather, as a daughter."

"Thank you, thank you," answered the young captain, pressing Lady Sophy's hand; "you know my feelings for your cousin, but to no one else would I venture to acknowledge them. To her I feel that I have no right to speak of them. I leave myself, therefore, in your hands."

"I trust to be so guided as to act for the best for you both," said Lady Sophy, "but I must not longer detain you. I hope that we may see you here again before many days have passed."

Well satisfied, as he had reason to be, with what Lady Sophy had said, Captain Denham followed his officers, who had already preceded him to the boats. He stepped in, and the order was given to shove off. The boats made the best of their way towards the corvette. The wind was already blowing strongly, and a heavy sea rolled into the bay.

"It is as much as we shall do, if we manage to beat out of the bay this evening," observed the lieutenant to the midshipman in his boat, "I ought to have kept my eyes more about me, though it is natural enough the captain's should have been preoccupied."

"Yes, sir, indeed that is a lovely girl, Lady Nora; he will be a happy man who wins her."

"That is a matter, Mr. Merton, too delicate for me to pronounce on," answered the lieutenant; "but I was speaking of the difficulty of beating out of the bay."

"Oh yes, sir, I beg your pardon," said the midshipman; "still I believe we shall be able to carry all sail, and if so, the *Ariadne* will soon find her way out of this difficulty."

"That is an ugly reef to the north," observed the lieutenant; "I would rather it were fifty miles away than where it is."

"Yet it affords us good shelter when the wind is as it was this morning."

"So it does," answered the lieutenant; "but it is directly in our way when we have to beat out when the wind is in the west."

The captain made no remark to the midshipman in his boat; he was too completely absorbed in his own thoughts, though he occasionally urged his crew to greater exertion by the usual exclamation of "Give way, lads, give way."

The boats were soon alongside. Directly they were seen coming, the officer in command had begun to get the corvette under weigh, and when the captain stepped on board the anchor was hove up to the bows.

The corvette, under top-sails and top-gallant-sails, was now hauled close to the wind. She cast to the north, and stood directly towards the reef of rocks which appeared ahead. The captain took his place in the weather rigging, to con her, while scarcely had sail been made on the ship before the increase of wind made it doubtful whether she would carry what was already set. The dark clouds came rolling up in thick masses from the west overhead, while heavy seas, topped with foaming crests, rolled in from the same direction. The corvette heeled over until her lee ports were in the water, still it was not a moment for shortening sail. Now the young commander gazed at the shore under his lee, now to the dark rocks ahead, and now at his masts and spars. "No higher," he had more than once to cry out, as the men at the helm, anxious to gain every advantage, kept her too close to the wind. "We cannot hope to weather the reef on this tack," he observed to the lieutenant, who was near him.

The crew were all at their stations, attentive to obey the least sign from their commander. Now a fiercer gust than ordinary made the ship heel lower in the water. Now she rose again. It was a critical moment as she rushed forward with headlong speed towards the threatening reef, over which the sea was always furiously beating. Still the young commander stood calm and collected. Now his hand was raised and as he glanced towards the helmsman, now he looked once more to the sails aloft. "Hands about ship," he shouted in a clear, ringing voice, which every man heard fore and aft. "Helm's a-lee! Tacks and sheets! Main sail haul!" It seemed as if in another moment the beautiful vessel would spring forward upon the threatening rocks. She was in stays, but the slightest shift of wind to the south would have driven her to destruction. Anxiously the commander looked at the fore-topsail still aback. For an instant the ship's head appeared not to be moving. Then gradually the wind forced her round. "Of all haul!" he shouted in a cheerful voice, as she sprang forward towards the opposite side of the bay. Still she was not free. The headway she made was counteracted by the heavy seas which now rolled in upon the land, and forced her towards it. Now she was standing towards Kilfinnan Castle. The commander turning, looked at the reef they had left; then once more casting his gaze ahead,—"We shall scarcely weather it the next tack," he said to himself. "If the wind holds as it does now, however, and if it does not increase much, the tight little ship will still work her way through it."

Anxiously those in the castle watched the progress of the corvette. They well knew the danger to which she was exposed, for although many a year had passed since any large ship had been cast away in their bay, yet there were traditions of men-of-war being driven on the coast and the whole of their gallant crews perishing. Numerous merchant vessels and smaller craft had also from time to time been dashed to pieces on the rocks, and many sad tales there were of lives being lost, when the persons, on board the vessels appeared within but a short distance of the shore.

Nora had sufficiently recovered to go to the window and gaze forth upon the vessel.

"O, what a beautiful fabric she is," she exclaimed; "how rapidly she draws near!" With the glass she could almost see those on board. "But will she, do you think, escape that reef to the north, when she once more tacks?"

"Oh, yes, I trust so," answered Lady Sophy, "he who commands on board is an experienced seaman, you know, and if any human being could carry the ship out of the bay, he will do so."

Besides the young ladies, several other persons on shore were watching the progress of the corvette, as she endeavoured to beat out of the bay. Far down below in the sheltered cove, in front of her cottage, stood Widow O'Neil. Her white locks, escaping from the band which generally bound them, streamed in the wind. The hood of her red cloak was thrown back, and while with one hand she steadied herself by one of the supports of the deep caves of the cottage, she stretched forth the other towards the ocean, as if she would direct the course of the bark which struggled through the foaming waves.

"They are brave men on board that craft," she exclaimed to herself, "but oh, it is hard work they will have, to get clear of the bay. Proud and trim as that beautiful ship looked this morning, who can say but what before another sun rises, she will be a shattered wreck upon yonder cruel rocks. Such a sight I have seen night after night as I lay on my couch, I know not whether asleep or awake; but, oh, may Heaven protect those on board from such a fate, if their vessel, stout as she may be, is thrown upon yonder reef.

"'My boy, my boy! Even now he may be on the stormy ocean, threatened with shipwreck, as are those in yonder beautiful vessel. May Heaven protect him and them!'"

As she spoke, the fish-wife stretched forth her neck more eagerly over the ocean, and again and again she offered up a prayer for the safety of those on board the ship which struggled below her. High up the glen, in a sheltered place, yet still commanding a view of the bay, sat another person. It was Father O'Rourke. He, too, was watching the ship, with a very different feeling animating his heart, to that which worked in the bosom of the widow. No prayer for the safety of those on board escaped his lips. He seemed to gaze with satisfaction on the fearful danger to which she was exposed. He more than once exclaimed to himself, "She cannot escape yonder rocks, and then that pert and daring youth who set me at defiance, with all his companions, will meet the fate which they and their Saxon countrymen so well merit. Curses on the heads of those who execute the behests of King George and his ministers. While we have red-coats and blue-jackets arrayed against us, what hope is there of liberty for old Ireland? I hate them all. From the king on his throne to the meanest soldier who trails a pike in his service!"

At a short distance, on a high and projecting part of the cliff, stood a wild and fantastic figure. It was that of mad Kathleen. She waved her arms round and round. Now she shouted, as if she would warn those on board the ship of the danger they were approaching. Again and again she cried out, as if encouraging them to perseverance in their bold attempt at beating out of the bay. Sometimes she uttered blessings on their heads, especially that of their young commander.

"A brave youth, a noble youth he is," she exclaimed; "even when I set eyes on him this morning I felt my heart drawn towards him. Grievous would it be for him to lose that fine ship, his first command, and still more grievous were his life to be taken by the angry waves!"

Thus she continued for some time, until she was interrupted by a hand being placed on her shoulder. She turned round and saw Miss O'Reilly standing near her.

"What, Kathleen, are you trying to show yonder ship the way to beat out of our bay?" asked Mr. Jamieson, in his usual kind voice.

"I would I were on board, minister, that I might help to guide them," she answered with a laugh. "There are many worse pilots than I am, and often in girlhood's days have I sailed with my father on yonder sea, sometimes, as now, tossed with waves, at other times calm and blue, like a young maiden's eye, void of guile and treachery."

"But, tell, me Kathleen, do you think the ship will manage to escape from the dangers by which she is surrounded?" asked Miss O'Reilly, in a somewhat agitated voice. "They say her captain is a brave and gallant officer, and it would be grievous if he were to lose that beautiful vessel, for so I am told she is."

"God who guides the winds and gives them power alone knows whether yonder ship will gain the open sea in safety," answered Kathleen; "but I will tell you, dear lady, if you stay by me, what progress she makes. If the prayer of a poor mad creature can save her, she is safe enough, and the wind will hold as it does now, sufficiently to the south to enable her to clear the reef. Oh, Miss O'Reilly, even now she seems rushing forward to destruction."

"Whereabouts is she?" asked Miss O'Reilly eagerly.

"Not two hundred fathoms, it seems at this moment from the reef," answered Kathleen. "If she can come about without difficulty, she will escape, but if not, in a few minutes she will be cast on the rocks, and then you know too well what will happen."

"Tell me, good Kathleen, tell me," said the blind lady, after a short silence, "has she gone about? is there once more a prospect of her escaping?"

"Again she is in stays!" exclaimed Kathleen. "See, see! the wind seems to have caught her. Oh, may merciful Providence watch over her! It seems to me that her head is once more turning towards the dreadful rocks. Alas, alas! no power can save her."

"Oh, may Heaven protect them!" exclaimed the blind lady, turning her sightless eyes in the direction of the ship. "Oh, may those brave men on board escape the fearful danger in which they are placed!"

"Your prayers are heard, lady! your prayers are heard!" shouted Kathleen; "the wind has taken her head-sails, and once more she is on the starboard tack, standing away from that fearful reef."

Mr. Jamieson and his niece stood for some time watching the progress of the corvette, till the shades of evening, increased by the thick clouds which obscured the sky, hid her from their sight; but they could not persuade Kathleen to leave the spot, for she declared that she could still see the ship through the mist. At length, the minister and his niece returned to their home, leaving poor Kathleen still wildly waving her arms and shouting, until her voice was hoarse, as if she would address those on board the vessel.

"See, see! she is once more about! Surely her bowsprit is pointing more seaward than it was before, and if the wind was to shift a little more to the south, she would soon be clear of yonder fearful reef."

The corvette once more going about, stood to the north. Although the wind might have drawn a little more to the south, yet this advantage was counter-acted by the fierceness with which it blew. The masts, with more sail on them than it would have, under other circumstances, been deemed prudent to set, bent with the unusual pressure. Sometimes, indeed, as Captain Denham gazed up at them, they seemed like fishing-rods, so fearfully did they bend before the breeze. The first lieutenant and master were also looking up at them with not less anxiety than did the captain. "They will scarcely stand this pressure," observed the former; "what say you, master?"

"We must keep the canvas set, at all events, and trust to Providence," answered the master. "This is no moment for taking in a reef. If they go and the ship refuses to stay, we must bring up, though I fear the little vessel will scarcely hold her own against the heavy seas which come rolling into this bay; and, to my idea, both she, and some of us on board, will leave our bones to rot on the strand under our lee, if it comes to that."

"Let's hope for the best, master," answered the first lieutenant. "See how calm our captain looks. You would never suppose that he is aware of the danger in which we are placed."

"He knows it pretty clearly, though," observed the master. "Hold on, good sticks, hold on," he exclaimed, looking up at the masts. "They are tough spars, I know, and they are now giving good proof of their quality."

Sometimes, from the direction of the vessel's head, it appeared possible that she might weather the reef towards which she was approaching. Then, again, she fell off, and it was evident that she must make another tack before there was a chance of her doing so. The commander seemed of this opinion, and was clearly unwilling to approach again as near as before to the reef. Again he shouted, "Hands about ship!" As before, the helm was put down, the tacks and sheets were raised, the men hauled with a will at the braces, and the ship's head, coming up to the wind, continued for some moments pointing west, to the open part of the bay. Anxiously the commander watched her movements. At one time it seemed as if she had got stern way, and he opened his mouth about to give the order to let go the anchor and to shorten sail. Those on board knew the order would have been followed by another, dreaded by all seamen—to cut away the masts, the only mode of proceeding to enable the corvette to ride out the gale. Again and again the captain looked up at the head-sails. "She is paying off!" he exclaimed. A shout, though immediately suppressed, burst from the throats of the crew.

For the moment they were safe, from the threatened danger. Again the corvette stood across the bay. The topmasts, as before, bent to the gale.

"We shall easily clear that reef," observed the master. "Well, it is a pleasure to see a man con a ship as our fine young skipper does. These are moments to try a man's mettle, and he has shown that he is of the true sort."

The corvette flew across the bay, almost, it seemed, with lightning speed, so soon was she again on the opposite side. Another critical moment had arrived, and it was only to be hoped that the gale would not come down with greater force than before while she was in stays, or very likely at that moment her topmasts would be carried away. Again about she came; this time without difficulty, and now her head pointing seaward, she stood out from the bay, still as those on shore watched her through the fast gathering gloom of evening, she seemed to be drawing nearer and nearer to the reef. Now once more she looked up to the west, then again to the north; still the masts and spars stood. Yet, after all, she was nearer the reef than under such circumstances a seaman would wish to find his ship.

"Mr. Matson," said the commander, looking down at his first lieutenant, "we must at once take two reefs in the topsails; but it is a risk for the hands aloft, a fearful risk indeed," he added.

"I am ready to lead the way, sir," exclaimed a young seaman, who was no other than Ned Davis, the commander's old companion.

"Give the orders then, Matson," said the captain.

"Aloft, there," shouted the first lieutenant, scarcely, however, had the men sprang into the rigging, when there was a loud crash. The main topmast had gone close to the cap. The straggling sail and wreck of the spars hanging over the side.

"Clear away the wreck," cried the captain. "Not a moment to be lost. We must save the other masts."

The men flew aloft, Ned Davis being among the first, drawing out their knives from their pockets as they did so. In a few seconds the ropes were severed, and the mast and spar fell overboard, with the still loudly flapping sail. At the same moment the crew throwing themselves out on the fore topsail-yard, that sail was quickly reefed. "You must take another reef in it, Mr. Matson," said the commander, "closely reef it, or that mast will go also." The mizen-topsail with greater ease was closely reefed. In consequence of the ship having been deprived even for that short time of the power which urged her through the seas, she had drifted down, it seemed, close upon the reef. Once more the captain looked anxiously to leeward.

"We shall still weather the reef," he exclaimed to the first lieutenant, who, after gazing at it, looked in his face as if to ask a question, "Unless," the commander added, "the wind draws more out of the west."

Heeling over, however, less than she had before done to the blast, her head pointed seaward, clear of the reef, still, should she be making much leeway, it would be doubtful whether, after all, she would clear it. To tack close to it, crippled as she was, would be dangerous in the extreme. The commander stood, as before, at his post.

"She will do it, Matson," he said, speaking to his first lieutenant.

"God grant she may," answered the officer.

On she flew. The sea dashed in masses of foam high above the dark rocks which formed the extremity of the reef. On, on, she stood. A few seconds almost would decide her fate. Many an eye glanced over the lee-bulwarks. The water washed up through the scuppers, and rose high on deck. The crew sheltered themselves as best they could under the weather-bulwarks, for the seas were breaking in masses of foam over the weather-bows, deluging the decks fore and aft.

The commander gazed also anxiously at the reef.
The corvette darted on. Already the foam which
flew over her seemed to unite with that which broke
above the rocks. Still, he did not turn pale, nor
did his eye quiver. In another instant she would
be hurled to destruction or be free. The crew
watched the threatening reef, and many an old seaman felt that he had never been in greater danger.

CHAPTER XVIII.

NED DAVIS, when he came down from aloft, had taken his post again near his beloved commander. "I am a good swimmer," he said to himself, "and I will do my best to save the captain. If I fail I will perish with him." Such were the thoughts which passed through his mind, as the most critical moment of all had arrived. Nearer and nearer the corvette drew towards the rocks. Now they appeared broad on the lee-bow—now they were right abeam—and at length many a bold seaman drew his breath more freely as they were seen over the quarter. The danger was passed. The beautiful little ship flew on, breasting bravely the foaming billows. At length she had clear room once more to make a tack. She came about before it might have been expected, crippled as she was, and now with her courses hauled up she stood out to sea.

"Pipe below," cried the captain, leaving the weather side of the poop, where he had stood since the ship had first got under weigh. "Keep her south-west Mr. Matson," he observed, as he retired to his cabin; "and call me on deck should any change take place in the weather."

It would be difficult to describe the feelings of those on shore who had watched for so long the manœuvres of the corvette as she worked her way out of the bay. Often Lady Nora lifted up her hands as if praying to Heaven for the safety of those on board. Each time, too, the ship approached the dangerous reef, with the character of which she was so well acquainted, her cheek turned paler than usual, and her bated breath showed the agitation of her feelings.

Yet, did she love the young commander of the corvette? She would scarcely have acknowledged thus much to herself. He had not declared his affection, and yet she felt almost sure that he was truly attached to her.

"I must remember that he was poor Barry's friend," she said to herself; "yet Barry did not pretend to know to what family he belonged; indeed, he would never tell us how he first became acquainted with him. That was very strange, for as often as I put the question he evaded it, and replied, 'I value him for himself, for the noble qualities he possesses, and not for what he may possibly have been. On board ship we think only of our rank in the service, and what sort of fellow a man shows himself to be by his conduct. So, Nora, do not say anything more about the matter.'"

At length, when the corvette, as far as she was able to judge in the thick gathering gloom of night, seemed to be clear of the land, Nora could not refrain from giving vent to her pent-up feelings in tears, while a prayer of thankfulness went up from her heart to Heaven.

Some time passed before she entirely recovered from the effects of the fearful danger in which she had been placed. She looked forward, day after day, for the return of the corvette, but in vain. She eagerly examined the newspapers, but none of them mentioned the *Ariadne*. She might still be on the coast of Ireland, or have been ordered elsewhere. From what Captain Denham had said before he took his departure, she was fully persuaded he would soon return; and it must be confessed, she longed to ask him many questions. There were various doubts passing through her mind which she was anxious to have solved. She scarcely, however, would trust herself to speak of them even to Sophy. She was soon to have her mind occupied with other cares.

Her father, who had never recovered the loss of his son, or his visit to the West Indies, was now

very evidently declining in health. He could no
longer follow the hounds, or ride out as before.
He took little or no interest in public affairs. Even
his neighbours he declined seeing when they called,
though he seemed always glad to have a visit from
Mr. Jamieson or his blind niece. He held frequent
conversations with the steward about his affairs,
which seemed greatly to trouble him. At length
it was determined to send to Dublin to request the
presence of his family lawyer, Mr. Finlayson, who,
though now an old man, was sufficiently hale to
undertake the journey. He had, it appeared, as
had his father before him, managed for many years
the Kilfinnan property.

Nora willingly agreed to write to request his
attendance, for she felt, that as he was a faithful
friend of her father's, he would certainly be a comfort to him, and might also be able to suggest a
means of placing the property in a more satisfactory state than it was in at present. She thought
nothing of herself; it scarcely occurred to her that
she was to become the heiress of it all. She knew
that the title would become extinct at her father's
death, but that caused her no regret. She supposed that her income would enable her and her
cousin Sophy to live as they had been accustomed.
More she did not require.

Within a week Mr. Patrick Finlayson arrived in a chaise from Dublin. In those days the journey was not performed as rapidly as at present, and the dangers to be encountered were not a few. He was a small, neatly made, active little man, with a clear complexion, which even his advanced age had scarcely succeeded in depriving of the hue of youth, though his hair was white as snow. His eyes were bright and intelligent, and his whole manner and appearance showed that he was still capable of a considerable amount of active exertion. His brown suit, knee breeches, and silk stockings, were set off by brightly polished steel buttons and diamond buckles. Having paid his respects to the ladies of the family, and addressed Lady Nora in his usual easy, familiar style, which showed that he had from her earliest youth claimed the honour of being one of her admirers and friends, he made more especial inquiries about the Earl.

"You will see a great change in my father," said Nora, "but your coming will, I feel sure, do him good. You know more about our affairs than we do. I only hope things are not worse than he supposes, and if they are, I must ask you to conceal the truth from him; I am afraid it would do him no good to make him aware of it, and would only deeply grieve him. I care not so much if I only am the sufferer."

"You need not be alarmed, my dear Lady Nora," answered the old man, taking her hand. "Things are not worse than the Earl supposes; on the contrary, I have of late seen the importance of not allowing him to believe that they were improving as much as they have been. You know probably, your good father's disposition, and are aware, that had he discovered this, he would very quickly have launched out again into his old habits of extravagance, which, however, from the sad account you give of him, he is not now likely to do, and therefore I am prepared to tell him the whole truth. Your affairs, Lady Nora, require nursing, I will confess to that, and careful management, but a few years of economy will, I hope, place them on a satisfactory footing."

"This is indeed pleasant news you bring us, Mr. Finlayson; I own when I heard that you had consented to come, that I feared things were rather worse than better, but I am indeed very grateful to you for coming; you have always been one of our truest friends, and I am sure at the present moment you will be a great comfort to my poor father. I will let the Earl know of your arrival, and I am sure he will be glad to see you at once. During the last few days he has grown very much weaker, and his medical attendant will not tell me what he thinks of his case. He himself speaks very willingly to our friend and neighbour Mr. Jamieson, who when I ask him what he thinks, always looks very grave, and replies, 'that the lives of all of us are in God's hands, and that we should be prepared to lose those we love at any moment.' This makes me, as you may suppose extremely anxious."

While Lady Nora was speaking the old gentleman became very serious.

"I should like to see the Earl as soon as possible," he observed; "I have several matters of importance to consult him about, which I should not like to put off until he becomes still weaker than you tell me he is at present. You will excuse me, Lady Nora, when I say I should like to be alone with him for some time."

"O yes, sir," said Lady Nora; "I know that whatever you have to say to my father you have the right to say to him; and I feel such perfect confidence in you that I have no desire to pry into any secrets you may have with him."

Nora having left the lawyer, soon returned with the information, that the Earl was ready to receive him.

Mr. Finlayson found the Earl sitting in an armchair, propped up with pillows, gazing out on the ocean on whose blue and slightly ruffled waves the sunbeams were playing brilliantly. The Earl smiled as his old friend entered, and held out his hand warmly to him.

"Sit down, Finlayson; you have come at a sad moment. I feel a strange weakness creeping over me, and I am glad that you have not longer put off your visit. Yes, I believe the moment is approaching for which we all should be prepared, when I must leave this world. I wish I could look back to all I have done during my life with satisfaction; but I cannot say that I can do that. I have been hospitable and generous, I own, according to the notion of people; but alas! Finlayson, for the peasantry under my charge, for the multitudes of my poorer neighbours, how little have I done? I might have set them a better example; I might have obtained some education for them; and, perhaps, by going among them, restrained them from committing the excesses into which from time to time they have plunged."

"Very true," answered the lawyer; "I believe there are very few people who have not to say something like that, when they are about to leave the world; but we must not think of what we have done or left undone ourselves. You believe in the simple Gospel; I am sure you do, or you would have listened to Mr. Jamieson's preaching, as I have often seen you doing—in vain. We will speak of that by-and-by.

I rather hope that you think worse of your case than you should do. I do not hear that the doctor is of the same opinion as you are, and so, my dear lord, there are certain points with regard to your property which I, as your legal adviser, would wish in the first place, to discuss."

Mr. Finlayson then entered into particulars, which it is not here necessary to introduce.

The Earl seemed much relieved on hearing that his property was less encumbered than he had supposed.

"But there is another point, my lord, on which I shall wish particularly to consult you."

"Well, the sooner we speak of anything of importance the better, Finlayson. We know not what another day may bring forth," observed the Earl.

He already spoke with some difficulty.

"Well, my lord, at all events I should like to know your wishes on the subject," said the lawyer. "Your lordship knows that your father had an elder brother."

"Yes," said the Earl, in a somewhat surprised tone.

"He was considerably older than your father," continued the lawyer. "He was a somewhat wild and extravagant man. Your lordship may possibly remember that he engaged in one of the unhappy outbreaks of those days."

"Yes, yes," said the Earl hastily. "I heard that he became a rebel against his king and country."

"Well, my lord, you know many honourable men joined with him on that occasion."

"I fancy that he was found guilty of high-treason, was he not?" said the Earl.

"Yes," answered the lawyer. "An act of attainder was passed against him, by which he lost both title and property. Had it not been for the interest of your father, it would have been lost to the family altogether; but, as he had always proved loyal, he was allowed to inherit the property in the place of his brother, for your grandfather, if you remember, was alive at that time."

"Yes; but of what consequence is that at the present day?" asked the Earl.

"I am coming to that, my lord," said Mr. Finlayson. "Your uncle, it appeared, married and had a son and your father, who really loved his brother, being at that time a bachelor, petitioned the Government, that in case of his death without an heir, his elder brother's guiltless child might succeed to the property, and regain the title of which his father had been deprived."

"Ah!" said the Earl, "I was not aware of that; but had this relative of mine (this cousin I suppose I should call him) a son?"

"That for a long time was a matter of doubt," said the lawyer. "It appeared, however, that he, when a young man, inherited many of his father's qualities, and was in all respects fully as wild and unmanageable as he had been, and he very soon, in consequence, brought himself within power of the law."

"I hope he never committed any act unworthy of a gentleman or of his name and family," said the Earl, with more animation than he had hitherto shown. "At least I trust one of the last scions of our race brought no disgrace on it."

"No, my lord," said the lawyer, smiling; "he was only guilty of that gentlemanly act,—treason, having united himself with some of those unhappy people, who hoped to overthrow the authority of the Government. He became a United Irishman, and took part in the rebellion of that time. He was at length committed to prison, and to my great dismay I found that he had been condemned to death."

"Did he retain his own name, or had he assumed another?" asked the Earl.

"He had some time before dropped his family name, and wisely too, considering the position in which he was placed," answered the lawyer. "He had contrived, however, to make friends both within and outside the walls of the prison, and by their means he managed to escape. A price was of course set upon his head, and it was generally supposed that he had left the country. I thought so likewise for some time; but his father, who was then alive, had placed some sums of money in my hands, and empowered me to devote them to his assistance. I suppose he discovered this, for after a short time I received a letter from him, by which he led me to understand that he was still in the country, but in a position where it was not at all likely he would be discovered. He told me, moreover, that he had no intention of leaving Ireland; that he had lately married a young country girl, and was very happy in his present position. He praised his wife as a most beautiful creature, and said that in her society he hoped in future to remain quiet, and refrain from any of the acts which had hitherto brought him into trouble. He had taken so many precautions that, notwithstanding all my exertions, I could not find out where he was. Still he enabled me to remit the money he required. I should have told you that when your father had made the arrangement which I have been describing, he bound over his nephew and his son not to make any claim to the title, as long as an heir of his own line existed. But should he have no male heir, then the eldest of his descendants was allowed to put in a claim for the title. This document, and other legal proofs of his identity, your cousin had obtained possession of. He told me, I remember, in his letter, that he considered himself strictly bound to adhere to the agreement, and that as for himself, he had no wish ever to claim the title which had belonged to his ancestors; that he had sufficient to satisfy his wants; that he was tired of ambition; and that he was perfectly content to let his country go on in its present condition, without interfering in politics. I replied that his resolution was a wise one, and undertook whenever he desired to have the money forwarded to him, to send it immediately. I of course did my best to try and discover where he was and whom he had married. Once or twice I was very near succeeding. I traced him to two or three places, but at length I entirely lost all clue to him. I suspect he was aware I was endeavouring to discover him, and thus, as he had already had much practice in playing the game of hide-and-seek, he was able completely to evade me."

"That is a strange story you have told me," said the Earl; "I had forgotten many of the circumstances to which you allude. Alas! as long as my own boy lived it was a matter of no consequence. I felt very sure that my own patent was secure,

and that he would inherit my title and estates;
but now it seems that through this curious arrangement of my father, matters have altered; but surely should an heir appear, he could not deprive my
daughter of Kilfinnan Castle, and the estates which
belong to it."

"In the unlikely event of a claimant establish-
ing his right to the earldom, he would also inherit the Kilfinnan estates," answered the lawyer;
"but you will remember there are the estates in
Derry, which were formerly separated from the Kilfinnan property, and according to the arrangements
made by the late Earl, they become the heritage
of the females should there be no son to succeed.
Thus Lady Nora will at all events retain the Derry
estates, even though it may turn out that your
long-missing cousin has left a son to inherit the
the title and Kilfinnan property."

The Earl sighed deeply.

"It matters very little to myself. My dear Nora
has no ambition, and as her tastes are simple, she
will be perfectly content with the Derry estates,
where she will, I feel sure, devote herself to the care
of the surrounding peasantry, and will avoid those
extravagances which would injure her property, as
alas! I have done."

The lawyer sat for some time longer with his

friend, but the Earl at length, observing that he felt very faint, desired that his doctor, who was in the house, might be sent for. The man of medicine soon appeared, and feeling the Earl's pulse instantly administered restoratives. In a short time the Earl rallied, and desired that Lady Nora and his niece might be sent for. They came and sat with him for nearly an hour, when he begged that they would retire to their rooms, assuring them that he felt much better, and that he hoped the following day he should have more conversation with Mr. Finlayson on the matters of business which he wished to discuss with him.

CHAPTER XIX.

EVENING approached, and Nora and her cousin sat in the tower chamber overlooking the ocean. They neither of them felt disposed to go to sleep. The night was calm and lovely, the atmosphere unclouded. The stars shone forth brightly, and the light crescent moon was reflected in the waters below. The reef of rocks on the other side of the bay could be distinguished, and the lofty headlands beyond it stood out in bold relief against the sky, while to their extreme right they could see the whole sweep of the bay and the lofty downs above it. It is not surprising that they should have been unwilling to tear themselves away from such a scene. It calmed their agitated feelings, for Nora could not conceal from herself that one of the kindest of fathers was about to be taken from her, while Lady Sophy, almost friendless as she was, felt that she was about to lose her best protector. She could, it was true, live on with her cousin Nora, and watch over her, as she had ever done, like an elder sister over one far younger than herself. Already, Lady Sophy's early beauty had completely departed. There was the same outline of feature, and the same elegant figure, but her countenance wore that sad expression (too often to be seen marking the features of the once young and lovely) of disappointed affection, of blighted hopes. Thus they sat on, hour after hour. A dark shadow passed across the moon, and threw a gloom over the hitherto bright landscape. Suddenly they were startled by a loud, wild shriek. It seemed to come from far away across the ocean. Now it swelled into a high note of wailing; now it sank into a mournful tone of grief. Again and again that strange sound struck their ears.

"The banshee!" exclaimed Nora, placing her hand on Sophy's shoulder with alarm. "Surely I have always believed that it was a mere superstition of the ignorant peasantry—a phantom of the imagination; but here is a dreadful reality. Yes, it surely must be the banshee, and what does it forebode? Sophy, you know too well, and so do I. Perhaps it is sent in mercy, to warn and prepare us for that dreadful event. But ought we not to have been prepared already? The last words my dear father spoke to me were sufficient to make me feel he was aware of the great change about to take place. Let us hasten to him. Perhaps even now his spirit is departing, and I would be at his side at that awful moment."

"Stay, Nora," said Sophy; "I do not believe in the banshee, or any other being of the sort. I see no figure, and even did I, I should not be convinced that it was a being of another world. I know that many believe such things exist. Some think they are sent in kindness; others, that they are rather evil spirits permitted to disturb the parting hours of the dying; but that, at all events, I am sure is not the case. Let us watch a short time longer. Depend upon it, we are deceived in some way."

"Oh, no, no!" exclaimed Nora, pointing towards the nearest part of the beach which was visible. "See that phantom figure moving across the sands! Surely that must be the banshee! What else?"

"No, dear Nora, calm yourself," answered Sophy. "Do not you recognize the figure of poor mad Kathleen? She must have uttered those cries as she passed under the castle walls. She must have come to ask after the Earl, and, as bad news flies fast, she has probably been told he is sinking rapidly. So, as she has received many a kindness from the family, she is giving vent to her grief in those wild, unearthly screams and cries."

"You are right, Sophy," answered Nora, "but, for the moment, I could not help believing in the existence of the wild phantom we have read of and heard so often about in our younger days from the surrounding cottagers. Yes, I see it is poor Kathleen. I trust my poor father has not heard it, for, in his weak state, it might have a bad effect upon his nerves. Yet he certainly does not believe in the existence of the banshee."

The poor girls had not long to watch before they were again summoned, and this time it was to stand by the dying bed of the Earl. Holding the hand of his daughter, which he gently pressed, he breathed his last, with scarcely a sigh, and evidently without any pain or suffering. Mr. Jamieson, who had been summoned, stood by him. "He rests in peace," he said; "he trusted in One all-powerful to save, though he made but little profession of his faith."

Poor Nora was led from the death-bed of her father to her own room, but it was long before she could find vent for her grief in tears. Her cousin Sophy had long ceased to weep. Those who have suffered great unhappiness, whose fondest affections have been blighted, as hers had been, often find it impossible again to gain relief by weeping. Such was her case. She mourned the loss of the Earl, as much as did her cousin, but it was in a different way. Not a tear dropped from her eye. She found no vent for all she felt. Nora, on the contrary, exhibited her grief far more violently, and thus, perhaps, the sooner regained tranquillity.

Mr. Finlayson, as he had promised the Earl, acted the part of a kind father to her. He treated her as a petted child, spoke words of comfort to her on all occasions, and tried by every means to raise her spirits. Often he succeeded in doing so, and she could not help expressing a wish that he could remain at the castle, instead of returning to Dublin.

"Well, well," he answered, "I will do my best to please you, my dear young lady. I have a son and grandson well able to attend to my business, and as long as I am not required at home, you shall have the benefit of my company."

In those days the burial of even a peasant was attended with much parade, and any family would have been thought mean unless the body of their deceased relative was properly waked. Although the corpse of a Protestant Earl had not to go through this ceremony, yet it would have been looked upon as a great disgrace to the family had not all the neighbours been invited from far and near to attend the funeral, and be sumptuously feasted. Had Nora been consulted she would gladly have avoided anything of the sort. Mr. Finlay-

son declared, however, that it was not the day to
break through their old customs, and, for the credit
of the family, they must issue the usual invitations.
Nora and Sophy, however, begged that they might
be allowed to keep their rooms, although Nora had
been anxious to attend her father to the grave.
This it was arranged she should do in a private
carriage.   When the day arrived, however, from far
and near came squires and squireens, and farmers
and peasants, in all sorts of conveyances, the larger
number being on horseback, while several friends
of the deceased nobleman arrived from a distance
to pay their last respects to his remains.

It was a sad sight, even to Nora; but she resolved
to go through with what she thought was required
of her, and then she hoped to be allowed to remain
at rest for many a long day.   The parish church, in
which the tomb of the family was situated, was
about three miles off; and after the guests had been
regaled at breakfast with wines of all sorts for the
upper classes, and whisky, which flowed in profusion,
for the lower, they mounted their horses, and entered
their conveyances, to follow the hearse decorated
with the usual trappings of mourning.   Behind the
hearse, in a mourning carriage, sat Nora and her
cousin, closely veiled.   Poor girls, how differently
they felt to the mixed multitude who followed them.

Their guests gave way to their usual habit of talking and laughing as they rode along. The events of the day were discussed. The good qualities of the late Earl; the prospects of his obtaining a son-in-law who might take his place and do the honours of the castle; the beauty of his fair daughter; and especially, the state of his finances. Few would have supposed that the lively and animated collection of men, who rode along in every variety of costume, were assembled there to pay the last honours to a deceased noble. They were silent, however, as they assembled round the grave. Some perhaps for the first time had then heard the burial service of the Protestant Church as a large proportion of the guests were themselves Romanists; some perhaps were struck with what they heard; others probably attended to little that was said. Nora and her cousin stood close to the grave, closely veiled as before; and as Nora gazed for the last time upon the coffin of her beloved father, her heart sank within her and she felt a longing to follow him to his quiet resting-place.

Again they made for the castle, and all restraint now being removed, laughing and joking was the order of the day. Some even, as the wine flowed faster, gave way to snatches of songs, while the last meets were fully discussed, and the prospects of the next year's harvest. It is scarcely necessary to describe the events which took place at the castle. A considerable number of the guests had no little difficulty in mounting their horses on their return home, from the generous liquor which they had imbibed out of the late Earl's cellars. Their great grief seemed to be, that there was no heir to succeed him, and to assist in keeping up the neighbouring hunt. At length the castle was once more at rest.

Mr. Finlayson set earnestly to work to arrange the affairs of the young heiress. The steward, and those who were employed by him, had generally acted honestly; but as he made inquiries about the tenants, many were in arrear with rent, and he saw that some effort must be made to compel them to pay. He called the steward in for a consultation.

"You give very good advice, Mr. Finlayson; but I will just ask you, as a Scotchman said, 'Who is to bell the cat?' You know, surely, that to attempt to distrain for rent on some of these gentlemen would assuredly bring a bullet through your brain or mine. It is not an easy matter to get money out of an Irishman when he is determined not to pay, and it is not for you or me, if we are wise men, to push the matter too hard. I will do my best and go among them, and put it to them, whether they would like to deprive the young heiress of her property. Perhaps, though they will not yield to force, they may to persuasion, and I am thankful to say, we still retain in old Ireland, the gift of blarney. You see, sir, we shall get much more out of them in that way. I will just ask them if they would like to attack a young lady and rifle her pockets. Put it thus to them, and show them that if they keep back the money they are doing the same thing. Now, we shall see, if I go on this plan, whether those who can pay will pay, while those who cannot pay, it is very evident, will not do so; but to my mind there is no use turning a man adrift in the world if you can help it. A better day may come, and then he may prove a good tenant. If you turn him out of one property he will just build a hut in another corner of the land, and you will have him there starving before your eyes, and you will not be the better for the move."

"Well, well, O'Connor, you are a wise man, I see. I will let you have your way in that respect. We will do nothing to create an ill-feeling against the dear young mistress, and it is for you and I who are engaged to serve her to look after her interests. I wish she had a good husband to help her; but it is my belief, from what I see here, that there is not a young man in the country at all fit for her. She is a good, gentle creature, and were she to wed one of the rollicking, harum-scarum young fellows who are her equals, he would break her heart; and stay-ing at home as she does, she is not likely to meet any others, while even abroad she saw no one to care for, or, at least, no one appeared, so perhaps she will continue to live a maiden life, and if so, she will require your assistance and mine as long as I remain in the world."

Nora and Sophy were relieved from much anx-iety by the continued residence of the kind Mr. Finlayson at the castle. He was so lively, so full of conversation and anecdotes, so kind and judi-cious at the same time. He raised their spirits more than any one else could have done. A young man would have been out of place. Even kind, gentle Miss O'Reilly, when she came over, though she talked very pleasantly, could do little to ani-mate them. Mr. Jamieson performed his part as well as he could, but he was not very animated; he was more inclined to speak in a serious than lively strain.

CHAPTER XX.

HAPPILY human beings are so constituted, that grief with few, especially with the young, lasts long. After a time, Lady Nora and her cousin recovered their usual spirits, and began to ride about the country as before. Their chief pleasure was to visit those they had long known, and to extend their search of others who might require relief. The surest means for those who are themselves in distress of obtaining comfort is to do good to their fellow-creatures. Several times they paid a visit to the old fish-wife, Widow O'Neil. She seemed to have grown more hardy and wiry than ever. It was wonderful what exertions she could go through. She often had the assistance of her brother Shane, who was, however, advancing in life, and not so active as before, while she appeared to have retained all her strength and activity. They remarked, whenever they paid her a visit, the delight she took in speaking of her long-lost son. She never failed to tell them that she had seen him in her dreams. She knew, she declared, that he was thinking of her, and though she could not say why he was detained, he was, she felt certain, endeavouring to come back to her. Sometimes she thought he was a slave in some foreign land; sometimes that he had been cast away on some desert island, and had to live there, unable to make his escape, and sometimes that he was in prison. She said she knew he was in far distant lands, as that alone would have kept him from her. They could not help being struck by the deep, the intense love and confidence in him which the old woman always expressed for her son, though they naturally had considerable doubts whether, if he really was alive, he could feel the same for her.

" He was a handsome youth," observed Lady Sophy to her cousin, but there was a wild, daring look in his eye, and he was a lad who, when once away, and having obtained a better position in life than that which he enjoyed in his early days, would very likely cast off all thoughts of his poor mother, and would have no wish to return to her humble cottage."

"Oh, no, no," said Lady Nora, "I could not think that of him; of course I do not recollect him clearly, except from the sketch you made of him, but yet I am sure from the expression of his countenance that he must have been as true and honest as he was handsome.   No, I would rather suppose that he has long since been killed.   Just consider how many thousands of seaman have lost their lives within the last few years in the numberless battles in which our country has been engaged, and how likely it is that he was among them, and that is why no one has received any tidings of him."

Such was the conversation which took place as they climbed up the hill to return to their horses. They had promised Widow O'Neil to visit her again in a day or two.   She had undertaken to supply them with shells which her brother Shane had collected, and which they wished to send to a friend at a distance.   When, however, the day arrived on which they were to pay their visit, the morning broke with a storm of rain and wind.   The dark clouds chased each other over the sky, and the wind whistled round the towers of the castle.

"It will be impossible for us to ride to Widow O'Neil's to-day," observed Sophy when they met at breakfast.   "I do not think Mr. Finlayson will promise to accompany us; he would not like to face the bad weather."

"Perhaps the rain will clear off, and then he will not mind the wind any more than we shall," observed Sophy.

Mr. Finlayson, who then entered the room, declared that should the weather clear, he was ready to mount the little cob which had been appropriated for his use, which was so steady, that occasionally the Earl had gone out shooting on its back, and so sure-footed, it had never been known to stumble.

"But, my dear Lady Nora, you must be more careful than you were once on a time, on a skittish young horse which nearly proved your death," observed the old lawyer. "A day like this tries an animal; and unless your steed is as steady as a rock I cannot sanction your going out."

"Oh, I will take care to ride one of the best behaved of our stud," answered Nora, "and Sophy shall have the next, as she is somewhat the better horsewoman. I am anxious to send off those beautiful shells to Miss Fitz-Patrick, as she particularly begged to have them, and we may not have another opportunity of doing so for some time."

It was thus arranged that the horses should be ordered in the forenoon, should the weather clear sufficiently, and that they would pay their visit to Widow O'Neil. In a short time the rain ceased falling, although the wind continued blowing as hard as ever; indeed, it was a complete summer gale. The clouds rushed rapidly along the sky, and the seas rolled in with all their force from across the wide Atlantic. It wanted an hour or more to the time they had agreed to set out, and the two ladies retired to their turret boudoir. Scarcely had they entered the room, when Lady Nora exclaimed that she saw a vessel in the north-west, at no great distance from the land. The glass was turned in the direction towards which she pointed.

"She is a large ship," she observed, "but she seems to me to have lost most of her masts, there is but one standing; yes, I am sure of that, all the rest are gone. With this fierce gale blowing on the shore, what a dangerous position she is in! I cannot make out what ship she is. Do you look, Sophy; what do you say to it?"

Sophy looked through the glass.

"I cannot make out to a certainty, but from her appearance, I should judge her to be a man-of-war. Yes, I am nearly sure of it; I should say that she is a frigate, for when I keep the telescope steady, I can almost count her ports."

Nora looked through the glass.

"Yes, you are right," she said; "she seems to be standing to the south, but she is evidently drifting fast towards the land. I see, though, she has got some after-sail set on the stump of the mizen-mast, and I think I understand it; she wishes to weather the reef, and of course after that take shelter in the bay. Yes, yes, that is clearly her object;

she is struggling bravely with the seas, but oh, in what fearful peril she is placed."

The ladies immediately ordered their horses round, proposing to watch the progress of the ship from the cliffs. "I daresay that Mr. Finlayson will not object to come with us at once," said Lady Sophy, and she left the room in search of him.

"Willingly, my dear young lady," he answered; "you will find that I am no despicable cavalier when once I am in the saddle."

The party were soon mounted and cantering across the downs in the direction of the struggling ship. Mr. Finlayson was much less acquainted with nautical affairs than were his fair companions, still he knew enough to be aware that the ship was in great danger. The wind prevented them from making rapid progress along the downs, although they urged on their steeds as fast as they could go, anxious to meet some one who could give them further information about the ship. They determined to go on till they reached the widow's hut, as they knew that, should her brother be there, as he had promised to be, they would learn more from him than from anybody else as to the probability of the ship escaping destruction on the dangerous reef towards which she appeared to be drawing. Still they hoped against hope, that she might struggle on and escape.   As they approached the end of the cliff above Widow O'Neil's cottage, they recognized her standing on a high projecting point of land, gazing towards the ship.   Her actions gave them the idea that she, like poor Kathleen, had lost her senses.   Wildly she waved her arm, sometimes clasping her hands, raising them towards heaven; then, again, she stretched them over the ocean.   As the ladies and Mr. Finlayson rode up to her, words of prayer were escaping from her lips.

"What is the matter, Mistress O'Neil?" asked Sophy, riding up to her.   "Why are you thus agitated this morning?"

"It is on account of a dream I had last night," she answered.   "That is no wonder, though, for every night as I lie on my bed I dream that my boy is coming back to me, though when I am about to clasp him to my heart he escapes away again; but last night I dreamed that he really had come back, and there he was lying in my arms, just as he was when an infant and smiling in my face.   He must come back soon, too, for I am getting old, very old, and oh, he will scarcely know me now!   There is not much time to lose; but he will come; yes, my lady, I know that he will come.   He will not be as young and beautiful, and strong, and happy as he was when he went away, so many, many years ago,—I know not how

WIDOW O'NEIL ON THE CLIFF.

many; I have lost all count of them. Oh, they have been years of grief and mourning to me—sad, sad years; but such have been the years of my life since one I loved was taken from me. Ah, if you had known him, ladies, you would have said I had reason to love him: and now, my boy, my only boy, to have been thus long kept from me! But he is coming back, ladies. I tell you, I dreamed last night that he was coming back; and suppose he was to be on board yonder ship! Ah, but I feel sure that he cannot be, for she will strike on yonder dark reef, and soon be a shattered wreck, to which no human being could cling and live. See how fiercely the seas roll in, and dash furiously over it! See, see how the brave frigate is drifting faster and faster towards the land! When I first saw her this morning she was a good two leagues away, and now there is not a quarter of a league between her and that rocky point. If once she strikes upon it, few of her sturdy crew will ever come ashore alive. Few, do I say? none, none can live amid those breakers. Oh, Heaven protect them!"

In spite of the strong gale which blew round them, neither the ladies nor Mr. Finlayson could tear themselves from the spot where they stood, it being the best situation they could reach for watching the progress of the labouring frigate.

CHAPTER XXI.

WE must for a time follow the fortunes of Charles Denham. Those were days of rapid promotion, when an officer's name stood well at the Admiralty. The young commander had not long served his time on board the corvette before he received his post rank. Scarcely twelve years had passed since he first stepped on board a man-of-war as a young seaman before the mast, when he found himself in command of a fine frigate of thirty-six guns—the *Isabel*. Ned Davis, who had followed him into every ship in which he served, now, by his advice, having applied for a warrant, was appointed boatswain to the *Isabel*. Although Denham had attained what might be considered the height of his ambition, he hoped while in command of the frigate, to make a still higher name for himself. Opportunities of doing so were not likely to be wanting. England had enemies in all directions, and there was every probability that a fine dashing frigate like the *Isabel* would soon meet with a foe well worthy of her. She was, however, much to the disappointment of her commander and crew, sent to the Mediterranean, which, by that time, had been pretty well cleared of all England's enemies. There was work however, to be done, and whatever Denham was ordered to do he performed it well. Having, at length, come home with despatches, he was sent to the West Indies, where he had already seen a good deal of service.

During this time he had few opportunities of hearing from the Earl of Kilfinnan, to whom, however he occasionally wrote, and got a kind answer in return. Again, after nearly four years' service, he was on his way home. When about three parts across the Atlantic, the weather for some time before having been very bad, a ship was reported right ahead. As the frigate approached her, she was seen to have her ensign downwards, as a signal of distress. She appeared to be a large merchantman. Her topmasts were gone, and she had, in other ways, evidently suffered from the heavy weather. As soon as the frigate drew near enough, she was hove to, and a boat being lowered, she was sent on board the stranger. As the officer in command of the boat stepped on board the ship, he was struck by the fearful appearance it presented. A few of the crew, pale and emaciated, were dragging themselves about the deck, scarcely able to stand upright, while on mattresses placed close to the bulwarks were numerous human beings, some apparently dead, others dying, moaning fearfully and in plaintive voices, petitioning for water.

It was a long time before the lieutenant could get any one to explain what had happened. The captain, it appeared, had died, and so had most of the officers and passengers. Their bodies had been thrown overboard. Great was his horror when he at length ascertained that they were suffering from the yellow fever. The weather was very hot, and it was but too likely even that this short visit to the pest-infested ship might cause him to convey it to the crew of the frigate. What, however, was to be done? He could not leave the unfortunate people on board the merchantman to perish by themselves, without help; while, should he remain, he and those with him might catch the same complaint. He found on inquiry that several persons were down below who had hitherto escaped the pestilence At length, uncertain how to act, he returned on board the *Isabel*, to receive instructions from his captain. The surgeon of the frigate was of opinion that the only safe plan was thoroughly to fumigate the vessel, and put a prize crew on board, to navigate her to an English port, as it would be unsafe to take any of the people out of her. This plan was followed, and an officer with twelve men went on board to carry the ship to Bristol.

It was hoped that from the short time the lieutenant and his men were on board no infection could have been conveyed from her to the frigate. Before two days, however, had passed these hopes were found to be fallacious. Two of the men who had been on board the merchantman were seized with the fearful complaint, and the following day were corpses. Several others in the course of a few hours were seized in the same manner. Their illnesses in each case terminated fatally. As is often the case, a panic seized the whole crew, and the men who would have faced an enemy boldly, trembled at the thoughts of the attacks of this unseen foe. The captain and officers had tried to encourage them and revive their spirits; but all seemed in vain. Not a day passed without several of the men being committed to the deep, and no one knew who would be the next victim. The surgeon declared his belief that the seeds of the disease must have been contracted in the West Indies, as it was impossible it could have been communicated by the people of the merchantman.

"Let the cause be what it may, the best hope we

have of getting free of the fever is to meet an enemy of equal size to ourselves; and, then, while we are fighting him, I have no doubt that 'Yellow Jack' will take to flight," observed the captain.

At length a breeze sprang up, and although the disease had not altogether ceased, it had considerably decreased. A sharp look-out was kept at all hours for any sail which might appear on the horizon. At length one was observed in the south-west, and all sail was made in chase. For some time probably the *Isabel* was not seen by the vessel she was chasing. The latter, however, was at length seen to make sail, and to stand away to the west. The *Isabel* was a fast vessel, and every effort was now made to increase her speed. The sails were wetted, every stitch of canvas she could carry was set, and every other device adopted to urge her through the water.

In those days the engagements which had taken place between English and French ships had terminated in most instances so disastrously to the latter, that Napoleon, it was said, had ordered all his cruisers to avoid fighting if they possibly could. This might have accounted for the flight of the stranger; for as the *Isabel* drew nearer, she was discovered to be either a heavy frigate or a line-of-battle ship. On a still nearer approach the French ensign flew out from her peak, and it was ascertained, without doubt, that she was a large frigate, a worthy antagonist for the *Isabel.* Superior as the enemy might be in guns and in number of men, Captain Denham resolved to attack her. The engagement he knew would be a severe one; but he trusted for victory to the tried gallantry of his officers and crew, and the resolution with which they would work the guns. He had the weather-gauge, and he hoped by skilful manœuvring to retain it. The enemy finding she could not escape, now hauled up her courses, and made every preparation for battle. The *Isabel*, when she drew near enough, at once opened fire to cripple her antagonist, and to retain the position she now enjoyed. This first broadside considerably cut up the Frenchman's rigging; but the fire the *Isabel* received in return did her still greater damage, badly wounding the fore-topmast. Davis went aloft to examine it, and reported on his return that he feared it would not stand much longer. Both the frigates now standing on a wind, continued to exchange broadsides; the English firing at the hull of their antagonist, while the Frenchman seemed to aim more particularly at cutting up the masts and rigging of the English ship.

"She seems to be full of men, and I suspect her

object is to get alongside, and to take us by board-ing," observed the captain to his first lieutenant.

"We will show them what British steel can do, if they make the attempt, sir," was the answer.

The Frenchman attempted to luff across the Eng-lish ship's bow, in the hopes of raking her, but Den-ham was too much on the watch to allow her to execute this manœuvre successfully. A consider-able number of the *Isabel's* men had been killed. Still, her crew fought on with undaunted courage. At length, her fore-topmast, which had before been severely injured by a chain shot, came down with a crash upon the deck. The Frenchmen shouted when they saw this, and another shout escaped them when they saw the main-topmast follow the fate of the other mast.

"If they attempt to run us on board we will try to secure them, as we did in the *Cynthia,*" observed the captain. "If we let a few of the Frenchmen come on board, we can quickly dispose of them, and then return the compliment."

"Ay, ay, sir," answered the lieutenant; "I will give the order to the men to prepare for boarding. They are ready enough for it."

Scarcely had he spoken, when the French frigate, luffing up ran her bows against the quarter of the *Isabel*. She was immediately secured there by Davis and others; and the Frenchmen came rushing over the bows, expecting to make her an easy prize.

"Boarders, rebel boarders," shouted the first lieutenant.

"I will lead you, my men," cried the captain, springing to the side.

A few Frenchmen who had gained the deck of the *Isabel* were immediately cut down; and now the English in turn swarmed over the enemy's bows. In spite of all opposition, they worked their way aft. No power seemed capable of resisting them. Although the Frenchmen for some time stood their ground, they were driven back. Step by step the British blue-jackets fought their way, and numbers sank before the sturdy blows of their cutlasses. Many of the Frenchmen were armed with pistols, by which several of the English were wounded. During this time Davis had ever kept close by the side of his commander. Captain Denham was leading on his men, when suddenly his cutlass dropped from his hand, and he would have fallen had not Davis supported him. At the same moment, a tall Frenchman, with uplifted cutlass, was in the act of bringing it down upon his head, when Davis, bringing his own weapon to the guard, saved his captain, and with a return cut sent the Frenchman reeling backwards.

"On, my lads, on," shouted the captain, again rising to his feet. "Though I cannot use my sword, you can keep yours going instead."

The energy with which he spoke was infused into his followers, and pushing onward they drove the Frenchmen before them. The Frenchmen, encouraged by their officers, attempted to rally; but no sooner had they done so, than, led by their gallant captain, the English made another dash forward, and again drove them back. Meantime, the weather had been changing, and the moderate breeze which had hitherto been blowing, was followed by a heavy gale. Although the *Isabel* was well-nigh dismantled, she was still more than a match for her opponent. In a short time, numbers of the Frenchmen having fallen, an officer was seen to run aft and haul down the French flag. The prize was won. She mounted four more guns than did the *Isabel*, with a far more numerous crew. The prospect of bad weather made it necessary at once to send a prize crew on board the captured frigate, and to remove the greater part of her own people, so that a few Frenchmen only were left on board. Great was the delight of the crew at finding, from the report of the surgeon, that their captain's wound was not likely to prove serious, though his arm might be disabled for some time.

The second lieutenant was ordered on board to

carry the prize into Plymouth, she having suffered but little damage in her rigging, while her captor was in a far worse condition. Some time was occupied in clearing away the wreck of the topmasts, and once more getting the ship into order. The gale, however, fearfully increased, and the frigate in an almost helpless condition, having lost sight of her prize, was driven towards the coast of Ireland. Happily, the yellow fever had completely disappeared; but Captain Denham had another cause of anxiety, lest his ship might be driven on that rocky shore on which so many a fine vessel has been lost. He anxiously looked out, therefore, for signs of the gale breaking, and that he might be able once more to make sail and beat off shore. His hopes, however, seemed likely to prove vain. The morning dawned, and far away to the east as the eye could stretch, appeared the high land of the Irish coast. He had hoped to have hauled up sufficiently to have weathered Cape Clear.

The gale continued till the frigate was close in with the coast. Shipwreck now seemed inevitable, for no other sail could be set to enable her to beat off shore. There was a bay to the south, but that would now afford no shelter, and no other harbour was open to her. It seemed impossible that she could be saved. One only resource remained, to anchor and cut away the masts. Orders were, therefore, given to prepare for this last alternative. The cables were ranged along the deck, and spare anchors got up from below. The dark seas came rolling in with unabated force from the west, while they broke with terrific force on the rocky shore under her lee. The spray dashed over her bows, flying fore and aft as she forced her way gallantly through the seas. The gale still continued with unabated force. Masses of clouds came rushing by overhead, rapidly succeeding each other, while under her lee-bow appeared a long reef of rocks, the dangers of which were well known to many on board. Still, hopes were entertained that she might be able to weather it. The eyes of the master and other officers, indeed of most on board, were turned now seaward, now to the rocky shore, and now to the reef on the lee beam. There seemed to all but little prospect, unless by a sudden change of wind, of being able to weather the latter.

"She would not stay if we were to attempt to go about," observed the first lieutenant, "and there is no room to wear, or it might be better if we were upon the other tack, so as to escape yonder threatening reef."

"We may possibly weather the reef," observed the master; "but if we were to attempt either to stay or to wear, we should inevitably be driven upon the rocks."

Several of the best hands were at the helm, watching for the directions of the master. Sometimes, after a slight shift in the wind, hopes were entertained that the reef might be escaped; but then, again, it was found she was making so much leeway that even this slight hope was abandoned. Onward she rushed to her inevitable destruction, it seemed. Meantime, the wounded commander had been lying in his cot. Several times he had desired to be carried on deck, but the surgeon, who sat by his side, entreated him to stop where he was, fearing the excitement would be too great, and that his wounds, which had hitherto been going on favourably, might take a turn for the worse.

"Then send the master to me," he said, "that I may learn the exact position of the ship."

The master made his appearance.

"I wish she was in a better position than she is, sir," he observed; "but we are doing all that men can do to claw off shore, and if we had had our topmasts, there would have been no difficulty about the matter. She makes fearful leeway, and there is an ugly reef ahead, which I do not altogether like; but I have been in as bad a case before and escaped, and I pray Heaven we may get clear this time."

"Doctor, you must let me go on deck, that I may see the worst. It is torture to lie here below," exclaimed the wounded captain.

"But the master says, sir, that we have a prospect of hauling off shore, and I again repeat that you would only incur great danger by exposing yourself to the cold wind and spray that you would have to encounter. No, no, sir; stay where you are, and let us hope for the best."

Many more anxious minutes passed. The master returned to his duty on deck, and the captain, having full confidence in his judgment, would not again send for him.

"Come, doctor, there are many poor fellows want your aid besides me; go and look after them, I entreat you," he said at length. "They will give me notice in time enough when all hope is gone, or, I trust, I may soon hear that the ship has weathered the reef, and has brought up in the bay."

Scarcely had he spoken when a loud roar of breakers reached even to where he lay. A cry arose on deck, and the next instant there came a fearful crash. The frigate had struck on the reef. The captain was endeavouring to rise from his cot, when Davis rushed into the cabin.

"It is a bad case, captain!" he exclaimed; "but

while I have life, you know I will stay by you. We are not far from the shore, and maybe, if the ship goes to pieces, some plank or timber may carry us there in safety."

Denham allowed himself to be carried on deck, where Davis secured him to the only portion of the wreck over which the sea did not break. The captain gazed around. The ship had struck upon the much-dreaded reef. Huge seas came rolling in, and, dashing against her with terrific force, had already begun to tear away her upper works, and it was evident she could not long remain in that position without going speedily to pieces. Many of the crew had already been washed away; others were clinging to different parts of the wreck. Some, including the officers, were endeavouring, not far from the captain, to form a raft, on which they hoped to reach the shore. It appeared, however, very doubtful whether they would succeed.

. "Let us chance it, sir," said Davis; "I will haul a grating here, and put you on it. Maybe, we shall be safely washed on shore."

"No, no, Davis," answered the captain faintly; "you remember how the brave Dutchman behaved when his ship was sinking. As long as two planks hold together I will stay by the frigate, or till every one has left her. You go, my friend; you are strong and unhurt, and, God protecting you, you may still save your own life."

"What? leave you, sir? leave you, Captain Denham?" exclaimed Davis. "I have not sailed with you for so many years to act thus at last. We swim or sink together. I have never feared death, and he is not now going to make me do a cowardly act."

"Well, well, Davis, I fear there is no use urging you. Perhaps, too, we run as little risk here as we should struggling in those boiling seas," said the captain.

"Right, sir; the frigate is new and strong, and maybe she will hold together until the gale somewhat abates," answered the boatswain. "I wish those poor fellows would stay on board with us; it might be the better for them."

"I would not order them to stay, Davis," answered the captain. "These seas, if they continue long, must break up the stoutest ship, and it is a fearful thing to have to struggle among floating timbers, washed about round such rocks as these."

While they were speaking, many of the crew, clinging to spars and planks, were seen drifting towards the shore. Few, however, appeared to reach it. Some, exhausted by their exertions, let go their hold and sank. Others were cast upon the reef, mangled fearfully by the timbers which were thrown upon them. The rest, meantime, continued to work at the raft. The surviving officers then came to the captain, and urged him to allow them to place him upon it, but he remained firm to his resolution.

"No, no," he answered; "do you leave the ship as you think best; but she was placed under my command, and nothing shall induce me to desert her as long as she holds together."

CHAPTER XXII.

MR. FINLAYSON and the two young ladies stood watching the progress of the labouring frigate.

"Heaven have mercy on them," exclaimed the Widow O'Neil, extending her clasped hands towards the ship. "See, see, she draws towards the reef! No hope! no hope! She has struck! she has struck!"

The fish-wife spoke but too truly. Fearful seas came rolling in, and, meeting with an opposition not hitherto encountered, dashed in huge masses directly over her. In another instant, the foremast, hitherto standing, tottered and fell. Stout as were her timbers, unable to resist such fierce assaults, they were in a brief space burst asunder, and scattered around in the troubled sea. A cry of horror escaped the young ladies as they witnessed the fearful catastrophe.

"Oh, how many brave men are at this moment carried into a watery grave!" cried Lady Sophy. Nora was silent. A fearful apprehension seized her.

"The last time we heard from Captain Denham, he told us that he was appointed to a frigate!" she exclaimed suddenly. "Oh, suppose that is the ship he commands?"

"Can no one go to the help of those poor men?" asked Mr. Finlayson. "Surely there are boats on the coast which might go off to them!"

The fish-wife turned as he spoke.

"There are boats, sir, but it would be hard to find the men who would venture off in such a sea as that; but if, as I believe, the wind is falling, there is yet some hope; if it goes down as rapidly as it sometimes does in summer, frail as are our boats, we may be able to reach the frigate."

The ship was too far off for those on shore to witness the dying struggles of those who were washed into the sea, but yet they could not tear themselves from the spot. Gradually the gale abated, seemingly contented with the mischief it had caused. Still, however, the seas rolled in with fearful force. Suddenly a thought seemed to seize Widow O'Neil.

"I must go, I must go!" she exclaimed. "If no men are to be found, I, at least, will go off!"

"Why, you would not venture out in such a sea as that?" cried Mr. Finlayson, calling after her as she began to descend the cliffs.

20

"That I will, sir, and go alone if no men will accompany me."

From the position of the coast in which the cottage was situated, it was easy to launch a boat, although the sea was agitated outside. On reaching her hut, the widow found her brother Shane standing outside it.

"Shane," she exclaimed, "you promised to stand by me on all occasions, now prove your words. I am resolved to go out to yonder vessel; there may be some alive on board. My heart tells me there are, and we must save them. O stir up some of the other men, and bid them follow us, if they are worthy of the name of men."

"I would go with you, sister," answered Shane, "if I could get others to go, but they will not raise a finger to save any on board a king's ship."

"But sure, they are our fellow-creatures, brother Shane," exclaimed the fish-wife. "Shame on the cowards if they dare not come, and shame on you, brother, if you will not help me. Listen now; I dreamed last night that he who has been so long away is coming back. It is not the first time I have dreamed it either, and you may say if you will, that this is only another fancy, but my days are numbered, and I know that before I die he will come back; he promised, and Dermot was not the

boy to break his word. Come, Shane, come. Look.
the sea has gone down, and you and I with your
boy Patrick, though he may have less sense than
other lads, will go off to the ship."

The widow's exhortations made Shane promise to
accompany her. Her boat was ill-fitted for the task,
yet for some distance they could pull out under shelter of a point which projected north of the cove.
As the wind had hauled round somewhat more to
the north also, it might be possible to set a sail, and
with less difficulty reach the frigate. Patrick was
summoned, and with his father and the fish-wife,
the boat was launched. She was cleared of all super-
fluous lumber, while Shane lashed under her thwarts
several empty casks, which would assist in giving her
buoyancy. It was a simple attempt at a life-boat, yet
with all these precautions, the old fishing craft was
but ill-fitted for the undertaking. The fish-wife again
and again urged her brother to hasten his work, so
eager was she to reach the wreck. At length the boat
was ready. The boy was placed at the helm, and the
fish-wife and her brother took the oars. They pulled
boldly out of the cove, and then along the shore for
some distance, where the water was rather smoother
than further out. Even there, however, the exertion
was considerable, and those who looked on from
above dreaded every moment to see the frail skiff

overturned by the rough seas. Now, however, the head of the boat was turned seaward. Shane and his sister increased their exertions. Often the waters broke on board, when Patrick, steering with one hand, bailed it out with the other; still they continued their course. At length they succeeded in gaining a considerable distance from the shore, when the seas, as is sometimes the case, came with less force, and gradually sank in height. There was only one point where they could approach the wreck. Just within sight was a small bay, or opening in the reef; the seas on every other side were dashing over the frigate, and would have immediately overwhelmed the frail boat. Bravely they rowed on, and they might have put to shame many of the sturdy men who had collected on the shore. Several times those who watched the progress of the boat from the cliff fancied she was overwhelmed. Now she sank into the trough of the sea, and the huge wave seemed about to dash over her. Again rising to the summit of a foam-crested wave, she was tossed for a few seconds ere she plunged into the watery vale below. More than once Shane proposed setting a sail, but the widow declared that her arms were still strong enough to pull the boat, and that it would considerably prolong the time before they could reach the wreck, as it would thus be impossible to make a straight course. She seemed, indeed, endued with super-human strength, for even her brother's arms began to fail him. Again and again she urged him to renewed exertions, with a voice tremulous with eagerness.

"We shall reach the ship before long—we shall reach the ship," she kept exclaiming; "row, Shane, row. Oh, brother, if you have ever loved me, do not fail me now."

Thus they continued rowing on. Not an hour before it would have been impossible for the boat to have made any progress; now, however, by the subsidence of the gale, the undertaking, though difficult and dangerous, was possible. As they drew near, even now several struggling forms were seen in the foaming waters, but ere they could reach them, one after another sank beneath the waves. A few, however were clinging to planks and spars, but the widow refused to go near them; it might have proved the destruction of the boat, had the attempt been made.

"They are floating, and will in time reach the shore," she said to Shane, "or if the sea goes down still more, we may return to pick them up. There are still some alive on board the ship; even just now, I saw an arm waving. Row on, row on, we may yet be in time—we may yet be in time."

The larger portion of the wreck had before this, however, been broken up, but the after-part and the starboard side of the quarter-deck remained entire. As the boat approached the wreck, broken planks and timbers continued to be washed away, till but a small portion appeared to remain.

By persevering efforts, the boat, however, drew nearer and nearer, avoiding, though not without difficulty, the masses of wreck which floated by. As the fish-wife and her brother looked up, they saw two human beings still clinging to the remaining fragments of the ship; one was waving his hand as if to urge them to greater speed. No other human beings were to be seen on board. A few had just before apparently committed themselves to a raft, and with this support were now approaching the shore. They had, however, passed at some little distance from the boat. Sea after sea rolling in dashed against the wreck, sometimes the spray almost hiding those on board from view. Larger and larger portions continued to give way; every sea which rolled in carried off the timbers or more planks from the sides. The boat was within fifty fathoms or so of the rocks, Shane looking out anxiously for any part of the wreck by which it might be approached with least danger. It seemed scarcely possible for them to get near enough to aid those on board.

"I fear, sister, we shall be too late," exclaimed Shane; "even now yonder sea which comes in looks as if it were about to tear the remainder of the wreck to fragments."

With a thundering sound the sea he pointed at broke against the wreck. In an instant the remaining masses of timber gave way, and were dashed forward into the boiling sea.

"Pull on, Shane, pull on," cried the widow. "I see two men still struggling in the waves; one is supporting the other, and guarding him from the timbers which float around."

"Which timbers may stave in the boat, and drown us all," observed Shane.

"No matter, Shane, pull on—pull on; let us not set our lives against those of the brave men who are floating yonder. What matters it after all if we are lost? Death can come but once to any of us." It is impossible to give the force of those words, uttered, as they were, in the native tongue of the Irish, which she spoke. "Pull on, Shane, pull on," again she cried. "Boy, steer for those men; see, they are still floating above the waves."

In spite of the masses of timber, which appeared to be thrown providentially on either side, the boat approached the two men, who still floated above the water.

"Save him, friends; never mind me," said a voice as they lifted the person he supported, and who, by his uniform appeared to be an officer, into the arms of Shane, he himself holding on to the gunnel of the boat. The officer was quickly placed in the stern sheets, when Shane helped his companion on board, and then again grasping his oar, pulled the boat safely round before the sea had time to catch her on the beam and overturn her.

The seaman hauled out of the water, the stimulus to exertion having ceased, sank down fainting by the side of his officer. The danger of returning was as great as that which they experienced in approaching the wreck. The spray flew over them, and it seemed that every billowy wave would overwhelm the frail bark. All this time they were watched eagerly by the young ladies and their old friend from the cliff above. On the boat came; now a vast sea threatened her with instant destruction, but the fish-wife and her brother, rowing till the stout oars bent with their exertions, urged on their boat and escaped the danger. Nearer and nearer she approached the shore; now a huge roller came thundering up close to her stern, and seemed about to turn her over and over, but it broke just before it reached her, and by vigorous strokes, forced ahead, she escaped its power. In another instant lifted on a foaming sea, she glided forward, arriving high up on the sandy beach of the little cove.

"There are two people in her," exclaimed Nora, who had been eagerly watching them. "We will go down and help them, for they evidently require assistance."

"Those two poor fellows must be nearly drowned," observed Mr. Finlayson, as he accompanied the ladies to the hut; "I wish we had a medical man here, but for want of one, I must take his place and prescribe for them. These fishermen are more likely to kill than to revive them by their rough treatment. Come, I will push ahead and try to save the men before they press the breath out of their bodies."

In spite, however, of the active movements of the lawyer, the young ladies kept up with him and they arrived in front of the cottage just as Shane and his son, aided by the widow, were lifting one of the men they had saved out of the boat. She insisted on taking the seaman first, and not till she had carried him up and placed him on her own bed would she help to carry the other. The lawyer, however, arrived in time to aid Shane in carrying up the young officer, for such he appeared to be. As soon as they arrived at the hut, the apparently drowned man was placed by Mr. Jamieson's orders in front of the fire, then, having taken off his coat, he knelt down and gently rubbed his chest. On the arrival of the young ladies, such blankets and clothes as the widow possessed were, by the lawyer's directions, placed to warm before the fire, that the half-drowned men might be wrapped in them. No sooner, however, did Lady Nora's eyes fall on the officer's countenance, than she uttered an agonized cry, and threw herself by his side.

"Oh, it is Captain Denham—it is Captain Denham!" she exclaimed, "and he is dead—he is dead." Pale and trembling she hung over him.

"No, my dear young lady," observed the lawyer, "he is still breathing, and I trust that he will soon recover,—I already indeed see signs of returning consciousness."

While Nora, regardless of all conventionalities, was assisting the lawyer and her cousin in rubbing the captain's hands and feet, the widow was bending over the inanimate form of the seaman.

"Shane," she exclaimed, "I told you my boy would come back, and here he is; I feel it, I know it. Oh, Dermot, Dermot, speak to me," she exclaimed. "Do not die now that you have come as you promised. Surely it is not to break your old mother's heart that you have just returned to die in her arms?"

Hearing these exclamations, the old lawyer turned round, and went to the side of the widow.

"You will be wiser, my good woman, if you were

to place some hot clothes upon his chest, and chafe his hands and feet, instead of calling out in that way. There is no fear about him; he has over-exerted himself, and his immersion in salt water has for the time deprived him of his senses; but stay, I see you have a kettle boiling on the hearth. It is time now to pour some hot whisky and water down his throat. As I left the castle, I took the precaution of putting a flask into my pocket." Saying this the kind old man mixed a mug of spirits and water, which he at once applied to the sailor's lips. It slipped without difficulty down his throat. The effect was almost instantaneous; he opened his eyes and looked around with astonishment.

"Dermot, speak to me, my boy, my own boy," exclaimed the widow in Irish, as she threw her arms around his neck.

"What does she say?" he asked, in a faint voice.

"Dermot, Dermot, speak to me," she again exclaimed, but this time she spoke in English.

"That is not my name, good mother," answered the seaman; "you must be mistaken; I am not your son. I never was in these parts before except once, when I came with my captain, though I have often enough been off the coast with him and others."

"Not my son—not my son," ejaculated the widow,

gazing at him, and putting back his hair, and again looking at his countenance. "Oh, how have I been deceived, and do you again say that your name is not Dermot O'Neil?" exclaimed the widow, wringing her hands, "and I thought I had brought my boy safe on shore, and that he was to be folded once more in his mother's arms. Oh, Dermot O'Neil— Dermot O'Neil, why are you thus keeping so long, long away from the mother who loves you more than her own life?"

The young officer, who by this time had been revived by the application of the good lawyer's remedies, now wildly gazed around him.

"That voice," he exclaimed, as if to himself; "I believed that she was long ago numbered with the dead, and yet it must be. Oh! mother, mother, I am Dermot O'Neil," he cried out to her, "your long absent son."

The widow rushed across the room, and putting aside those who kneeled around him, she threw herself by his side.

"You Dermot, you my son Dermot?" she exclaimed, looking at him. "Oh, how could I for a moment have been deceived?" She bent over him, and pressed many a kiss upon his brow. "Yes, those eyes, I know them now, and those features, too; I cannot again be deceived. No, no; see, here

THE RECOGNITION.

is the sign by which I should have known him, even though he had been given back to me as I dreaded, a lifeless corpse. But my Dermot is alive, my Dermot has come back to me." As she spoke she drew back the sleeve of his shirt, and there upon his arm she exhibited the blood-red cross with which her son had been born.

During this scene, the countenance of Lady Nora exhibited many changes; now a deadly pallor overspread her face, then again the rich blood rushed back from her heart. Still she kneeled by Captain Denham's side. His strength gradually returned, and supported in the arms of the old fish-wife, he sat up. His face was turned away from Nora, and his eyes rested on the features of the former. He took her hand between his.

"Mother," he whispered, "I have been cruelly deceived. The only letter I received from my native land told me that you were dead, and from henceforth I felt the tie which had bound me to it was severed. Once I returned to it, and my fondest wish was to visit again the cottage where I was born, made sacred to me because it had been your dwelling. I was prevented from carrying out my intention, and from that day to this I have never had the opportunity of returning, but the life you have saved shall be henceforth devoted to watching over you. I have gained fame in my profession, and I prize it, but it is nothing compared to the joy of being restored to you. Oh, mother, I have loved you as a son should his parent who has loved him as you have done me."

"Dermot, my boy, dear Dermot, I never doubted your love. I have always said that you were true and faithful, and now you have proved it; but, my son, I shall not long require your care. My days are numbered; but I knew that you would come back, and I was not deceived. My prayers were heard in spite of all the threats and curses of Father O'Rourke. Now I have pressed you to my heart once more, and when I have seen you strong and hearty, I shall be content to place my head under the green turf and sleep in peace."

During this scene Lady Sophy and the lawyer had retired to the further end of the hut. Mr. Finlayson had, in the meantime, suggested to Shane, that he might assist the seaman, who was earnestly inquiring for his captain.

"It is all right," he exclaimed, when told that Captain Denham was doing well. "Heaven be praised that he is saved, when so many fine fellows have lost their lives. We were sadly short-handed on board the frigate, or I do not believe this would have happened; but the gale was cruelly against us. Are we the only ones who have escaped from the wreck?" "I hope not," answered Shane. "I saw a raft drifting towards the bay with several people on her, and many more may have been washed on shore on planks and spars."

"Then we should be up, and go and help them," exclaimed Ned Davis, endeavouring to haul on his wet jacket. "Are we to let our shipmates perish and lie here idle? It is not what the captain would have thought of; and if he had not been wounded he would have been up now, and looking out to help them."

This was the first intimation Mr. Finlayson had that Captain Denham was wounded.

"Why, that must be looked too," he observed. "Really, I do not think he can be attended to properly in this hut. We must manage to get a litter of some sort to carry him to the castle."

This remark was made to Lady Sophy. She appeared to hesitate

"What will Nora say?" she observed.

"Say! my dear lady! What possible difficulty can there be about the matter," exclaimed the lawyer.

He might not have interpreted aright the agitation exhibited by Lady Nora on discovering the parentage of the rescued officer.

CHAPTER XXIII.

WHEN, however, Mr. Finlayson's proposition was made to the fish-wife, she at first refused to agree to it, declaring that her son would recover as rapidly in the hut as he could in the castle; but on the lawyer's assuring her that she was mistaken, she consented to let him be removed if he wished it.

"Let me ask him then," said Mr. Finlayson.

For after Ned Davis had vacated the widow's bed, Captain Denham (for so he must still be called) had been placed on it. In the meantime, knowing that the fresh air would benefit Lady Nora, her cousin had led her to the front of the hut, and made her rest on a bench which was fixed there. Sitting down by her side, she took her hand.

"Nora," she said, "this is a strange tale we have heard. I can scarcely believe it. What do you think?"

"I know not," answered Nora faintly. "But can it be possible that he (Captain Denham I mean) whom we have known so long, who is so refined, so high-born in appearance and manners, can be the son of this wild-looking and ignorant fish-wife ? and yet, Sophy, she claims him as her son, and he does not deny it; and you observed that mark upon his arm; when she saw it, all doubt vanished. Oh, Sophy, help me, guide me, advise me. What can I do ? I did not know till now, when I thought him lost and then had him thus suddenly restored to life, how deeply I loved him. I tell you this, dear cousin, but I would not utter it to any other human being; but what can he be to me for the future ? My heart, I feel, will break, Sophy."

"Trials are sent us for our good, Nora," said her cousin. "Once I might have thought as you do, that unless his birth was high and noble, equal to your own, no man was worthy to become your husband; but, Nora," and Lady Sophy heaved a deep sigh, "I have learned to prize a true and noble heart; and if such is his, I cannot tell you that I believe you would be right in discarding him on account of his birth. This is not worldly advice; but I again repeat that I believe, if he is what we have all hitherto supposed him, there is not sufficient cause to refuse him as your husband."

Nora threw herself into her cousin's arms.

"Oh, thank you, thank you, dear Sophy," she exclaimed. "You are right. It was a fearful

struggle; but I should have died had I been compelled to give him up. I feel how cruel, how wrong
I should have been. I know he loves me, and
what a bitter feeling it would have caused his
noble heart."

"Then, Nora, let me go in and tell him that we
beg he will come to the castle. I am sure, that
without your invitation he would not consent to
be removed there."

"Oh, yes, do, do," exclaimed Lady Nora. "It
will be dreadful for him to have to remain here;
for his poor mother would certainly not know how
to take proper care of him."

While this conversation was going on, Mr. Finlayson had despatched Shane and Ned Davis, who
insisted he was now strong enough for anything,
followed by Patrick, with all the ropes and spars
they could collect, to go along the beach and assist in the rescue of any of the seamen who might
still have escaped drowning, and be even now reach-
ng the shore. He himself, meantime, undertook
to ascend the cliff, and send the groom back for
a litter on which to carry Captain Denham to the
castle. At first, when the proposal was made, he
declined leaving his mother's hut, and it was not
till her entreaties had been joined to those of Lady
Sophy he consented to place himself in their hands.

"You would greatly disappoint my cousin Nora if you refuse to comply with her request," whispered Lady Sophy.

It is possible that this remark might have settled the question.

"But does she know who I am?" he asked in a low trembling voice.

"Yes, yes," answered Sophy. "Do you suppose that to a true-hearted girl as she is that would make any real difference? Oh, Captain Denham, ask your own heart. Would you thus be ready to sacrifice any one you loved?"

"May Heaven reward her," he murmured.

His feelings seemingly overcame him, for he could say no more.

A considerable time elapsed before the arrival of the litter. Meantime Shane and Davis, with their young companion, hastened along the shore. Several other persons having seen the wreck had now collected on the beach. A few, fastening ropes round their waists, bravely rushed into the surf to assist in dragging the floating men on shore. Some, however, it was very clear, were more eager to obtain any articles of value that might be washed up than to save human life. Many were thus employed when Shane and Davis appeared. Several persons were seen clinging to the masses of wreck, which, after having been tossed about for a considerable time in the bay, were now being washed ashore. The glitter upon the jackets of two of them showed that they were officers, and several persons, as they drifted near, rushed into the water to assist them, so it seemed. They brought them safely up the beach, but no sooner were they there, than, instead of rendering them further assistance, they began to rifle their pockets, and to take their watches and the rings from their fingers. Davis caught sight of them as they were thus so eagerly employed as not to observe his approach. He dashed forward, and with a blow of a broken spar which he had seized, he knocked aside two of the wreckers, and so ably did he wield it, that he put the rest to flight before they could secure their booty. The rescued officers were two midshipmen of the ship, and their first inquiry was for their commander.

"He is all safe, sirs," exclaimed Davis. "Heaven be praised for it, but he was very nearly gone; however, it will not be long, I hope, before he is well again. It has been sad work; not a third, I fear, of our poor fellows have come on shore."

"Not so many, I am afraid," observed one of the midshipmen; "however, now we are safe ourselves, let us try to help others."

Several of the better disposed of the people now joined themselves to Shane, and prevented the wreckers from continuing their barbarous proceedings. A raft approached near the beach, and though perhaps none on it would have been saved, had they not had assistance, by the aid of the strong body of men who rushed into the water, all were safely landed before it had the opportunity of turning over upon them. Many dead bodies were cast ashore, and they were gradually collected and placed side by side. There were officers and men, and several poor boys, and a few of the marines. The survivors were undecided what to do when Mr. Jamieson, who, hearing of the wreck, had come down to the beach, invited them to the vicarage, and the bodies of the drowned were conveyed by his direction to the church. Before the shipwrecked men had proceeded far towards the vicarage, a messenger overtook them, from Mr. Finlayson, with a request that they would all come to the castle, to which their captain was now on his way. Every preparation was made for their reception. The medical man of the neighbourhood was also sent for, that he might attend to the captain and others who might have been injured. Fortunately, the surgeon of the frigate had also escaped, and he was at once able to look to the captain's wound. Lady Nora felt a strange satisfaction at having all those belonging to the frigate thus collected beneath her roof. She had a trial to undergo; it was when at length the Widow O'Neil desired to speak to her.

"Oh, Lady Nora," exclaimed the old woman, "I have discovered what I little thought of. My bonnie son loves you, lady. It may be presumption on his part, and it makes me feel more and more that I am not worthy to be his mother, but I am, believe me, his true mother. It seems strange that the son of one like me should thus have gained such a name as he has, but there is one thing I would tell you, lady, I know my days are numbered. You will not have the old fish-wife as your mother; if I thought so, I would gladly take myself away where you would never see or hear of me more. I would not stand between you and my son for all the world can give. You will not send him from you, lady?"

"Oh, do not speak thus, Mistress O'Neil," exclaimed Nora, rising from her seat and taking the widow's hands in hers. "I do not deny that I love your son, for long I have done so, though only this day have I discovered how deeply I loved him. My delight and satisfaction will be to save you from any further toil and trouble. You have ever proved a loving mother to him, and it shall be our united happiness to care for you, and to shield you from all the troubles and hardships to which you have been so long exposed. We will have a suitable house prepared for you and your brave brother Shane and his son, where you may live in comfort without toiling any more on the treacherous ocean."

"You speak like a true and noble girl," exclaimed the widow, "and now there is a secret I have got to tell you. If my son had not been restored to me, it should never have passed my lips, but I have long had in my keeping some papers, preserved in an iron case. It has been hidden under the floor of my hut, for I believe there are those who would deprive me of them if they knew where they are. Alas, I could not read them myself, but he who has gone, the father of my boy, bade me carefully keep them. To-morrow, lady, if that good gentleman who is with you, will come with the steward to assist him, I will place the case in his hands. If you had not confessed to me what you have now done, that my son is dear to you, I believe the contents of that box would have caused you much annoyance and pain, but now I feel it will only make you glad."

Lady Nora would thankfully have obtained more information from Mistress O'Neil, but she either would not or could not give it.

"In a few days I trust, in God's mercy, my son will have recovered, and then it may be time enough for you to examine the papers in the case," she answered. It was with difficulty that the old woman could be persuaded to occupy a room in the castle. She consented, however, to do so, when Shane promised to return to the hut and take charge of it till the next day.

The following morning Mr. Finlayson set forth accompanied by Mrs. O'Neil, for her cottage; Shane was watching for them. The widow sent him for a spade, and some minutes were employed in digging, before the promised box was discovered, so deeply down in the earth had she hid it.

"Ah," she observed, as her brother was working, "it was Father O'Rourke who had an idea of this case, and I could not tell what use he might make of it, if he ever got hold of it, and he who has gone charged me never to let it pass out of my hands."

At length an iron case was brought to light, which Mr. Finlayson attempted eagerly to open.

"I have never seen the inside of it," observed the widow, "and I do not know either how to get at it; but don't look at it here, Mr. Finlayson, carry it to the castle, where you may look into it at your leisure."

Mistress O'Neil having a few arrangements to make before leaving her hut, promised to follow Mr. Finlayson to the castle. The lawyer, on his arrival, after examining the case for some time, not unaccustomed to the various devices employed for such purposes, discovered the spring by which it was opened. The whole evening was employed by him in looking over the documents with which it was filled, but he declined for the present to explain their contents to Lady Nora, assuring her that they were somewhat complicated, and that unless he had examined them thoroughly, he might mislead those whom they chiefly concerned. To no one else, indeed, did he divulge their contents for several days; by that time Captain Denham was once more able to appear in public. Several guests had been invited to the castle, Mr. Jamieson and his niece being among them. They were all assembled in the drawing-room, when the lawyer, as the captain entered the apartment, went up to him and in a significant manner, took him by the hand.

"I have to congratulate you, my dear lord, on obtaining a rank of which you are—"

"Do you address me?" exclaimed Captain Denham with surprise. "What, my dear sir, do you mean? You do not intend to mock me!"

"I mean that you are the lawful Earl of Kilfinnan," answered the lawyer in a positive tone, as if his word had been called in question. "Although the elder members of your family were deprived of the right to assume the title, as long as another branch existed, I have sufficient evidence to prove that in your generation the attainder has been removed. Your father, the husband of the devoted woman whom you have always known as your mother—as she truly is—was, while living in the character of a fisherman, drowned off this coast. He was the grandson of the former Earl."

Captain Denham, or rather the new Earl of Kilfinnan, cast a glance, beaming with happiness and satisfaction, towards Lady Nora.

"Yes, indeed our kind friend, Mr. Finlayson, is not mistaken," she said, taking his hand, "and though you know full well my dear lord, that had it been otherwise, I had promised to become your wife, yet I rejoice to know that you can feel yourself with regard to rank in every respect my equal."

It is not necessary to describe the happy marriage which afterwards took place. The Widow O'Neil enjoyed the comfort and luxuries which had been prepared for her by her affectionate children but for a few months. Her nervous system had received a shock it never recovered, in the exertions she made in rescuing her son, but she had the satisfaction of knowing that she had saved his life, and that he was restored to the position his ancestors had enjoyed. He did not neglect his noble friend, Ned Davis, who continued, as before, his constant attendant, and ultimately, when he gave up the sea and came to live on shore, rose to the rank of his head bailiff. Mr. Jamieson and the kind-hearted lawyer both lived to an old age, and soon after her uncle was removed from her, his blind niece was laid to rest in the churchyard by his side.

Father O'Rourke went plotting and scheming on to the end of his days, and if he did not die in the odour of sanctity, having partaken of all the rites of his Church, no qualms of conscience that he had not exactly fulfilled the duties of a mission-ary of the gospel, seemed to have disturbed his last hours.

FINIS.